The Outsiders

This volume traces the unique trajectory of *The Outsiders*, from beloved book to beloved movie. Based on S.E. Hinton's landmark novel, Coppola's film adaptation tells the story of the Greasers, a gang of working-class boys yearning for security, love, and acceptance in a world ruled by their rival gang, the rich Socs.

The Outsiders: Adolescent Tenderness and Staying Gold explores the cultural impact of Hinton's book, the process by which Coppola made the film, the film's melodramatic components, the marketing of the movie to a young female audience, and the nostalgia industry that has emerged around it in recent decades, thereby illuminating how *The Outsiders* stands apart from other teen films of the 1980s. In its depiction of the emotional rather than sexual lives of young men on film and its recognition of the desires of teen girls as an audience, *The Outsiders* distinguishes itself from the standard teen fare of the era. With seriousness and sincerity, Coppola's film captures the essence of the oft-repeated, timeless message of the story: 'Stay gold.' This volume engages with a wide range of disciplinary approaches – film studies, gender studies, and literary and cultural studies – in order to distinguish *The Outsiders* as the significant contribution to youth culture that it was in the early 1980s and continues to be in the twenty-first century.

The book fills a gap in existing scholarship on youth culture and is ideal for scholars, students, and teachers in youth cultures, young adult literature, film studies, cultural studies, and gender studies.

Ann M. Ciasullo is a professor of English and Women's and Gender Studies at Gonzaga University, Spokane, WA, USA. She has published essays on bromance films, the television series *Mad Men*, 1980s nostalgia on Netflix, and humor and feminism in *MAD* magazine. This is her first book.

Cinema and Youth Cultures
Series Editors: Siân Lincoln and Yannis Tzioumakis

The Cinema and Youth Cultures engages with well-known youth films from American cinema as well as the cinemas of other countries. Using a variety of methodological and critical approaches, the series volumes provide informed accounts of how young people have been represented in film, while also exploring the ways in which young people engage with films made for and about them. In doing this, the Cinema and Youth Cultures series contributes to important and long-standing debates about youth cultures, how these are mobilized and articulated in influential film texts and the impact that these texts have had on popular culture at large.

Lady Bird
Self-Determination for a New Century
Rob Stone

Mustang
Translating Willful Youth
Elif Akçalı, Cüneyt Çakırlar, Özlem Güçlü

Mary Poppins
Radical Elevation in the 1960s
Leslie H. Abramson

The Outsiders
Adolescent Tenderness and Staying Gold
Ann M. Ciasullo

American Graffiti
George Lucas, the New Hollywood and the Baby Boom Generation
Peter Krämer

For more information about this series, please visit: https://www.routledge.com/Cinema-and-Youth-Cultures/book-series/CYC

The Outsiders

Adolescent Tenderness and Staying Gold

Ann M. Ciasullo

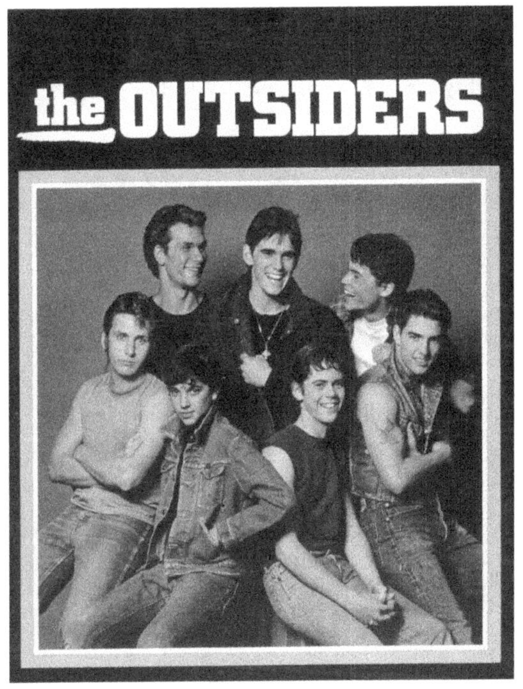

Poster for *The Outsiders*

Image courtesy of Warner Bros/Kobal/REX/Shutterstock

LONDON AND NEW YORK

First published 2023
by Routledge
4 Park Square, Milton Park, Abingdon, Oxon OX14 4RN

and by Routledge
605 Third Avenue, New York, NY 10158

Routledge is an imprint of the Taylor & Francis Group, an informa business

British Library Cataloguing-in-Publication Data
A catalogue record for this book is available from the British Library

Library of Congress Cataloguing-in-Publication Data
Names: Ciasullo, Ann M., author.
Title: The outsiders : adolescent tenderness and staying gold / Ann M. Ciasullo.
Description: New York : Routledge, 2023. | Series: Cinema and youth cultures | Includes bibliographical references and index. | Identifiers: LCCN 2022048942 (print) | LCCN 2022048943 (ebook) | ISBN 9781032133386 (hardback) | ISBN 9781032133393 (paperback) | ISBN 9781003228783 (ebook)
Subjects: LCSH: Hinton, S. E. Outsiders. | Hinton, S. E.--Film adaptations. | Outsiders (Motion picture : 1983) | LCGFT: Juvenile delinquency films.
Classification: LCC PS3558.I548 O9835 2023 (print) | LCC PS3558.I548 (ebook) | DDC 813/.54--dc23/eng/20221222
LC record available at https://lccn.loc.gov/2022048942
LC ebook record available at https://lccn.loc.gov/2022048943

ISBN: 978-1-032-13338-6 (hbk)
ISBN: 978-1-032-13339-3 (pbk)
ISBN: 978-1-003-22878-3 (ebk)

DOI: 10.4324/9781003228783

Typeset in Times New Roman
by MPS Limited, Dehradun

For Scott, my Tulsa boy

For Lori, still tuff as ever

And for my mom, Colleen, with gratitude and love

Contents

Figures

Series Editors' Introduction

Despite the high visibility of youth films in the global media marketplace, especially since the 1980s when Conglomerate Hollywood realized that such films were not only strong box office performers but also the starting point for ancillary sales in other media markets as well as for franchise building, academic studies that focused specifically on such films were slow to materialize. Arguably the most important factor behind academia's reluctance to engage with youth films was a (then) widespread perception within the Film and Media Studies communities that such films held little cultural value and significance, and therefore were not worthy of serious scholarly research and examination. Just like the young subjects they represented, whose interests and cultural practices have been routinely deemed transitional and transitory, so were the films that represented them perceived as fleeting and easily digestible, destined to be forgotten quickly, as soon as the next youth film arrived in cinema screens a week later.

Under these circumstances, and despite a small number of pioneering studies in the 1980s and early 1990s, the field of 'youth film studies' did not really start blossoming and attracting significant scholarly attention until the 2000s and in combination with similar developments in cognate areas such as 'girl studies.' However, because of the paucity of material in the previous decades, the majority of these new studies in the 2000s focused primarily on charting the field and therefore steered clear of long, in-depth examinations of youth films or was exemplified by edited collections that chose particular films to highlight certain issues to the detriment of others. In other words, despite providing often wonderfully rich accounts of youth cultures as these have been captured by key films, these studies could not have possibly dedicate sufficient space to engage with more than just a few key aspects of youth films.

In more recent (post-2010) years, a number of academic studies started delimiting their focus and therefore providing more space for in-depth examinations of key types of youth films, such as slasher films and biker films or examining youth films in particular historical periods. From that point on, it was a matter of time for the first publications that focused exclusively on key youth films from a number of perspectives to appear (*Mamma Mia! The Movie*, *Twilight,* and *Dirty Dancing* are among the first films to receive this treatment). Conceived primarily as edited collections, these studies provided a multifaceted analysis of these films, focusing on such issues as the politics of representing youth, the stylistic and narrative choices that characterize these films and the extent to which they are representative of a youth cinema, the ways these films address their audiences, the ways youth audiences engage with these films, the films' industrial location, and other relevant issues.

It is within this increasingly maturing and expanding academic environment that the **Cinema and Youth Cultures** volumes arrive, aiming to consolidate existing knowledge, provide new perspectives, apply innovative methodological approaches, offer sustained and in-depth analyses of key films and therefore become the 'go to' resource for students and scholars interested in theoretically informed, authoritative accounts of youth cultures in film. As editors, we have tried to be as inclusive as possible in our selection of key examples of youth films by commissioning volumes on films that span the history of cinema, including the silent film era; that portray contemporary youth cultures as well as ones associated with particular historical periods; that represent examples of mainstream and independent cinema; that originate in American cinema and the cinemas of other nations; that attracted significant critical attention and commercial success during their initial release; and that were 'rediscovered' after an unpromising initial critical reception. Together these volumes are going to advance youth film studies while also being able to offer extremely detailed examinations of films that are now considered significant contributions to cinema and our cultural life more broadly.

We hope readers will enjoy the series.

Siân Lincoln & Yannis Tzioumakis
Cinema & Youth Cultures Series Editors

Acknowledgments

There are many people who helped to make this book possible, but none more so than the editors of this series, Yannis Tzioumakis and Siân Lincoln. This is my first book project, and I could not have asked for a better experience. From start to finish, they have been encouraging, supportive, patient, and generous. Thank you, Yannis and Siân.

My university and colleagues have been incredibly supportive as well. Thank you to the Provost's Office and the Dean's Office of the College of Arts and Sciences for research funding for this project. I also owe an enormous debt of gratitude to the Interlibrary Loan staff at Foley Library; without their dedication to helping me gather sources both accessible and obscure, it would have been nearly impossible for me to write this book. The librarians at Bowling Green State University likewise played a crucial role in providing me with access to key archival materials, and I am grateful to them for their help. Finally, I am deeply appreciative of the encouragement I received from the English Department and from my close colleagues and friends at Gonzaga: Ingrid Ranum, Colleen McLean, Cindy Stavrianos, Suzanne Ostersmith, and especially my personal cheerleaders, Heather Easterling and Kris Morehouse.

So much of this book was enriched by talking to the many people either involved in the making of *The Outsiders* or committed to preserving the film's legacy. Thank you to Jo Ellen Misakian, Danny Boy O'Connor, Donnie Rich, Randy Shanofsky, Michael Fellwock, Dana Wirth Ludwig, James Mockoski, Timothy Shary, and Katie Sawyer for their generosity to me and their contributions to this project. Thank you to S.E. Hinton for writing the book that changed my life and Francis Ford Coppola for making the movie that defined my adolescence.

One of my biggest supporters was my mother, Colleen. Midway through the process of writing this book, she died very suddenly, leaving an enormous hole in my life. Though she wasn't familiar with *The Outsiders*, she always asked me how my project was coming along. She understood how important it was to me, and I am grateful for that. I am likewise grateful for the support of my siblings Lori, Tony, and Lisa. Finally, at the center of my life are the people who best know what this project has meant to me, and without them I wouldn't have made it to the finish line. Thank you to Laura Read, Brad Read, Oscar Orme, and Scott Orme for inspiring me to stay gold.

Introduction

The 1980s, *The Outsiders*, and Me

The date was 25 March 1983, a Friday night I had been feverishly awaiting for months on end. My 17-year-old sister, Lori, who had a license, a car, and a Pat Benatar style of cool, had offered to take me and my friends to the Garland Theater for the premiere of director Francis Ford Coppola's highly anticipated film adaptation of *The Outsiders*. I was 13 – one year younger than the film's protagonist and narrator, Ponyboy Curtis – and in my small world of St. Paschal's Catholic School in Spokane, Washington, I was indisputably the biggest fan of S.E. Hinton's novel. I was also unquestionably the school's authority on the movie, even though it had not yet been released. In the months leading up to the film's debut, I purchased every issue of *16 Magazine*, *Tiger Beat*, and *Teen Beat* with Matt Dillon, Ralph Macchio, and C. Thomas Howell on the cover. With their promise of insider knowledge of the movie and their delicious glossy fold-out posters of the actors, these magazines gave me the opportunity to build my expertise. I cut out images from them and plastered my PeeChee folder with the faces of Matt, Ralph, Tommy, and the cast so I could gaze upon them every day at school. In preparation for the film, my friends and I all adopted the names of the characters. Karen, sweet and bookish, was Ponyboy; Colleen, sensitive and innocent, was Johnny; Mary, tough and a little reckless, was Dally; and for reasons I do not understand to this day, I was Sodapop. We wrote notes to each other using these names, telling each other to stay gold. When the day finally rolled around, we could barely contain ourselves. We were not just going to see any movie; we were going to see the defining movie of our adolescence.

That Friday afternoon, Karen and Mary came over to my house to get ready for the event. We curled our hair and shellacked it in Aqua Net, carefully applied our 'Sugared Violet' CoverGirl eyeshadow, and kissed my full-size poster of Matt Dillon before piling into my sister's

DOI: 10.4324/9781003228783-1

VW Van. Before the movie, Lori took us to a throwback burger joint, Corky's, for fries and chocolate shakes, thus adding to the celebratory feel of the evening. And then it was finally time: time to buy our tickets, take our seats, and watch the film unfold. We went to the 7:30 p.m. showing, and the movie cost $3.25 – I know this because I still have my ticket stub – and I vividly remember the moment when the lights dimmed and Ponyboy's voice softly spoke the opening line of the movie: 'When I stepped out into the bright sunlight from the darkness of the movie house [...].' I had been waiting for so long, and it was finally here: Ponyboy's innocent face, Johnny's plaintive eyes, Dally's smoldering presence, and the energy of all the boys on screen – boys who lived with and for each other and who loved each other. Rapt, I sat as still as possible in my seat. I knew the whole story and I knew how it ended, but I also knew that I could not miss a moment of the film. To do so would be sacrilege.

When the film credits concluded and the lights went up in the theater, I felt a mixture of wonder and confusion. First and foremost was wonder, because all the still images I had devoured for months had finally come to life before my eyes, and they were gorgeous. Dally in a brown leather jacket, slouched against a lamppost and lighting his trademark cigarette; Cherry, immaculate in her powder blue sweater and preppie plaid skirt, confessing to Ponyboy, 'Things are rough all over'; Johnny, propped up against the park fountain, shivering in the cold night air and gripping a bloody knife while whispering, 'I killed that boy'; a tow-headed Ponyboy reciting 'Nothing Gold Can Stay' to Johnny against an impossibly amber landscape. The lushness of these images was such that they eventually became the ones I pictured every time I read the book again, and for the first and only time in my life, I did not mind that the actors cast to play the characters in the film replaced the way I had originally created those characters in my own imagination. But paired with relief was my other emotional response, one that I found odd and unsettling: confusion. I loved the actors and the gorgeous images on the screen, but something about the movie as a whole left me disappointed. Something was missing. Like the opening of the novel, when Ponyboy leaves the movie theater alone and is jumped by the Socs. Why did the movie not begin with this scene? And why had some parts of the story been left out, like the courtroom hearing, and the scene when Sodapop bolts from the house after begging Ponyboy and Darry not to fight? I loved Hinton's novel so much that maybe it was too much to ask the movie to measure up to it.

Twenty years later, I would discover that in fact the movie, in its original form, *had* measured up to the novel. Some of the very scenes

I had wondered about, as well as several others, had been cut from the film due to studio pressure to keep the running time under two hours; per the studio executives, anything exceeding ninety minutes 'was too long for a youth-oriented movie' (Phillips 2010b: 198). In 2005, Coppola released a special edition DVD entitled *The Outsiders: The Complete Novel* in which he restored them.[1] Even as a longtime fan of the movie, watching this edition was a revelation: it was the film I had wanted to see as an adolescent, one that fully reflected the narrative of the novel. Still, my viewing of *The Outsiders: The Complete Novel* was preceded by having seen the 1983 version a countless number of times. In my teenage years, I watched it anywhere and any way I could: first on cable TV, then on VHS in the mid-1980s, when it could be purchased for under 20 dollars. I still have that tape, well-worn from repeated use. Despite my mixed emotions on the film's opening night, I loved *The Outsiders*. By the time I was sitting in fifth row of the Garland Theater anxiously awaiting the opening credits, it had already become a part of me.

In the years that followed the release of *The Outsiders* I discovered other teen movies that spoke to me more immediately and urgently, likely because they were set in the present, not in the past – and likely because the present in which I was living, the mid-1980s, was what Elissa H. Nelson identifies as 'the most prolific period of teen filmmaking in the US' (2019: 1). Nelson observes that 'teen films made up approximately one of every ten films produced throughout the decade and an average of one of every five to six of the top fifty grossing films per year' (2). Coincidentally, I was the exact age of the protagonists in virtually every John Hughes movie, and as such, the female teenage angst exemplified by Molly Ringwald in *Sixteen Candles* (1984) felt like a reflection of my high school life. So, too, did the depiction of social cliques in *The Breakfast Club* (1985) and teenage whimsy in *Ferris Bueller's Day Off* (1986). Around this same time, my sister introduced me, via VHS, to *Fast Times at Ridgemont High* (Heckerling, 1982), her favorite movie in high school, which felt at once scandalous and thrilling in its unabashed depiction of youthful debauchery. In his book *Teen Movies: American Youth on Screen*, Timothy Shary explains how 'the 1980s teen witnessed a complexity of moral choices and personal options on which the multiplex movies thrived' (2005: 55). Every one of these movies capitalized on this complexity in some way, and being a confused teen myself, I became utterly engrossed in them. And the world that these movies portrayed was markedly different from the landscape of Tulsa, Oklahoma in the 1960s, where nary a high school dance, locker room, or party figured in the lives Ponyboy, Johnny, and Dally. To imagine them in any of these scenarios was absurd.

The incongruity of the image of Ponyboy and Johnny hanging out poolside, smoking pot with cute girls, underscores just how much of an outlier *The Outsiders* is among the canon of 1980s youth movies – and explains in part why it occupied a wholly different emotional space for me than the more popular and iconic '80s teen films. A quick glance at some of the titles released around the same time as *The Outsiders* makes this point even more compellingly. In 1982, the top teen films in the U.S. box office were *Porky's* (Clark), *Friday the 13th Part III* (Miner), and *Fast Times at Ridgemont High* ('Domestic Box Office for 1982' no date); in 1983, months after *The Outsiders*, both *Risky Business* (Brickman) and *Porky's II* (Clark) were huge hits ('Domestic Box Office for 1983' no date).[2] The following year, the release of *Sixteen Candles* marked the start of John Hughes's tremendously influential run as a 1980s Hollywood teen movie auteur. Though quite different in terms of content and character development, these films all have an investment in the standard themes of 1980s teen movies: sex, romance, drinking and/or drugs, and teenage immaturity. The same cannot be said for *The Outsiders*. While made in the 1980s and featuring up-and-coming stars of the era, very little of the film thematically reflected that era. In many ways, it was out of time, an anomaly. Which raises the question: in what way is *The Outsiders* a teen movie? How does it work within the conventions of the genre, and how does it work against them? Nelson argues that teen films of the 1980s 'focus on universal cultural problems central to the genre: How do teens navigate the coming-of-age process and become self-actualized? How do they find their place in the world, one that has been damaged by the previous generation, while retaining a sense of themselves and being true to their values?' (2019: 11). On the one hand, *The Outsiders* clearly engages with the coming-of-age experience, particularly through its protagonist, Ponyboy. On the other hand, it does so through narrative and cinematic conventions that distinguish it from virtually all other 1980s teen movies. This very distinctiveness – borne in part from the origins of the film – is the focus of this book.

The enduring success of *The Outsiders* and its portrayal of adolescent coming of age cannot be understood without first understanding the fertile ground from which it sprang: S.E. Hinton's 1967 novel. Written when she was only 16, *The Outsiders* was informed by her own life experiences growing up in Tulsa, Oklahoma. Drawing on previously published interviews with Hinton as well as reviews and critical analyses of the novel, Chapter 1, 'The Life and Legacy of S.E. Hinton's Novel,' provides readers with an understanding of both how popular and how impactful the novel was upon its publication in the U.S., and how its influence continued to be felt in subsequent years. When it was first published, the novel was lauded for its gritty realism and authentic narrative voice, and it is now widely identified (alongside *The Catcher in the Rye*) as having inaugurated the Young Adult (YA) genre. In the 15 years between its initial publication and its adaptation into a film, *The Outsiders* maintained a high profile due to its presence in middle- and high-school curricula in the U.S. An analysis of its characterization and themes will be central to my later examination of the film, particularly given that Hinton was deeply involved in its production – an experience she says ranks 'among the best' of her life (quoted in Michaud 2014). Indeed, Hinton served as a special consultant on the set, a role she was invited to undertake with the film's world-famous director, Francis Ford Coppola.

Coppola, reeling from the critical and commercial disaster of *One from the Heart* (1982) and the impending bankruptcy of Zoetrope Studios, saw *The Outsiders* as an opportunity to return to the smaller, more personal filmmaking experiences that preceded *The Godfather* series (1972, 1974) and *Apocalypse Now* (1979) – an opportunity 'to forget [his] troubles and have some laughs again.' Coppola likened the experience to summer camp and saw his role as that of 'camp counselor' (quoted in Harmetz 1983). In both the casting and filming of *The Outsiders*, Coppola created an atmosphere in which the young cast was encouraged to be young. Chapter 2, 'Francis Ford Coppola and *The Outsiders*: Famous Director Turned Camp Counselor,' thus explores two interrelated topics. First, it situates *The Outsiders* within the arc of Coppola's career in the 1970s and 1980s. Given that the film follows both his biggest critical successes (*The Godfather* films, *Apocalypse Now*) and his biggest critical and commercial blow (*One from the Heart*), it is crucial to explore not only why Coppola landed upon *The Outsiders* as his project but also what he hoped to achieve through the film, especially given that teen films are typically not the purview of esteemed auteurs such as Coppola. In an interview about the movie, he expressed his interest in stories 'about young people and about belonging' (quoted in Chaillet and Vincent 1984: 93), an investment exemplified by his following *The Outsiders* with another Hinton adaptation, *Rumble Fish* (1983), and three years later with his much more critically and commercially successful film, *Peggy Sue Got Married* (1986). The second thread in this chapter thus explores how his interest in and keen understanding of youth culture – particularly in the casting and production of *The Outsiders* – contributed to his success in cultivating a supportive, dynamic environment for the cast.

Coppola said that one of the things that drew him to *The Outsiders* was its theme of young people longing for a sense of 'belonging to a peer group with whom one can identify and for whom one feels real love' (quoted in Chaillet and Vincent 1984: 93). That Coppola used the word 'love' is significant, insofar as a simple plot summary of *The Outsiders* would not immediately reveal the role that love and affection play in the story. These themes, however, emerge powerfully in the film adaptation. Unlike other entries in the 1980s teen film genre, *The Outsiders* is not about romance, sex, drinking, or the yearning for a boyfriend or girlfriend; it focuses instead on the camaraderie and tenderness between young men. By privileging the emotional (rather than sexual) life of young men, *The Outsiders* is a teen film unlike most others of the 1980s. Chapter 3, 'Form and Feeling in *The Outsiders*,' explores its uniqueness through a two-pronged analysis of the film. First, I examine the film's relationship to its cinematic predecessors and influences, most notably *Rebel Without a Cause* (Ray, 1955), so as to underscore the distinctiveness of *The Outsiders* on the early 1980s Hollywood teen film landscape. Then, I bring a gendered lens to bear on the film, demonstrating how its cinematography, composition, and narrative align it more with the genre of melodrama than with a typical juvenile delinquent teen film. Coppola himself even described *The Outsiders* as 'a melodrama with a romantic tone' (quoted in Thomson and Gray 1983: 61), a description that invites a consideration of how his representation of adolescent masculinity runs counter to the gender norms of the era. As a whole, this chapter emphasizes *The Outsiders'* distinct vision of male youth culture, especially as it emerges in Coppola's 2005 re-issue of the film.

Another significant way in which Coppola's film engaged with youth culture was in its casting and subsequent marketing. In a 2014 interview, Hinton observed that 'one of the things that makes [*The Outsiders*] work is that the boys were very close to the same age as the characters' (quoted in Michaud 2014). She contends that in our current era, studios 'would be casting [adults] to play these little kids' (ibid., brackets in original). In truth, studios were casting adults to play kids well before *The Outsiders*; one need only look at the 1978 box office smash *Grease* (Kleiser) for illustration. Yet Hinton's observation invites further exploration, and in Chapter 4, '"Matt, Ralph & Tom Will Make You Cry": Critical and Popular Responses to the Film,' I examine how the casting and performances impacted the film's reception among two diametrically opposed groups: Anglo-American film critics and readers of U.S. teen magazines. The title of this chapter comes from a December 1982 cover of *Tiger Beat Star*, a popular U.S. girls' publication at the time. Months before the release of the film, the magazine hyped the emotional impact of the film as well as the attractiveness of its stars, most of whom (except for Matt Dillon and Diane Lane) were relative unknowns at the time. Inviting young female viewers (assumed to be heterosexual) to dream about the possibility of romance with Matt, Ralph, and Tom (Howell, not Cruise), these magazines played a major role in promoting the film before its release. Their enthusiasm for *The Outsiders* stands in contrast to the contempt for the film expressed by critics, almost all of whom dismissed the movie as overwrought, unrealistic, and, in its representation of affection among the boys, uncomfortable. The cultural zeitgeist around *The Outsiders* both before and upon its release must be examined in order to understand the film's contribution to youth culture – in the 1980s and now alike.

The Outsiders spoke powerfully to a youth audience upon its release, and in the nearly 40 years that have since passed, it continues to do so. Its enduring popularity is the focus of Chapter 5, '"Stay gold, Ponyboy": Nostalgia, Fandom, and *The Outsiders*.' In 2017, Tulsa hosted a 50th anniversary celebration of Hinton's novel, and C. Thomas Howell and Ralph Macchio attended one of the main events. Around the same time, Rapper Danny Boy O'Connor, a former member of the hip hop group House of Pain, purchased and restored the house that was featured in the film, opening 'The Outsiders House Museum' in Tulsa in 2019. The Museum exhibits paraphernalia from the movie, including Johnny's switchblade and Coppola's director's chair, and hosts hundreds of visitors every weekend. In this chapter, I explore the fan industry around *The Outsiders* as exemplified in The Outsiders House Museum, an industry in part fueled by nostalgia. Informed by interviews with O'Connor as well as other people involved in the day-to-day workings of the Museum, I discuss how and why the house has become a mecca for fans of Hinton and the film alike. In doing so, I consider the role that different kinds of nostalgia play in creating and sustaining this market. And as we fast approach the 40th anniversary of the film in 2023, the Conclusion, 'The Legacy of *The Outsiders*,' reflects upon the ways in which the book and film continue to speak to twenty-first century audiences. From the burgeoning popularity of the Museum and its vibrant fan culture to the upcoming stage musical based on the novel and film, *The Outsiders* has proven to be a story for the ages, one that speaks to old and young alike.

The subtitle of this volume – 'Adolescent Tenderness and Staying Gold' – bespeaks the twin affective prongs of *The Outsiders*: the feelings of affection and emotional honesty that often accompany the experience of being young, and the desire to protect and maintain those feelings in the face of the realities of impending adulthood. So many teen films are borne out of this complex and often overwhelming tension between childhood and adulthood, but many of these same films rely on the conventions of the genre to mitigate the seriousness of the experience. In his landmark study of teen films, *Generation Multiplex: The Image of Youth in American Cinema since 1980* (2014), Timothy Shary identifies four subgenres of youth cinema since 1980: youth in school (e.g., *Fast Times at Ridgemont High*), youth romance (e.g., *Porky's, Risky Business*), youth horror (e.g., *Friday the 13th*), and delinquent youth (a category in which he places *The Outsiders*). In the early 1980s, all four subgenres thrived, and while most of their representative films acknowledge the challenge of adolescence, they do not allow the weight of it to define their narratives. High school films and raunchy comedies tend to belie or downplay the genuine difficulty of one's teenage years as a liminal emotional space; slasher films exaggerate this difficulty to the degree that it becomes a site of terror – something horrifying, but unrealistically so. Even the juvenile delinquent film, exemplified by *Rebel Without a Cause*, leans into exaggeration and problem-solving, often at the expense of genuine feeling. What characterizes *The Outsiders* as an outsider in the 1980s teen genre is its sincere, authentic attitude toward the emotions felt and expressed by the characters in the film. While I am in no way saying that it was the only authentic teen film of the 1980s – to be sure, *The Breakfast Club* perhaps holds the honor for the most realistic and searing portrayal of teen angst – I contend that no other teen film of that era combines authenticity with a most rare theme in the 1980s, and one that I explore throughout this volume: the importance of non-romantic love and tenderness among boys. 'Unlike the cheap and often vapid teen tales that were plentiful then,' Shary observes, '*The Outsiders* had an entirely professional sheen, with such a confident production design, and such a serious and timely story […] about loyalty among men' (2022). I agree with Shary but would argue that, more accurately, the film is about loyalty among *boys*, and in highlighting the provisional and vulnerable nature of their boyhood, *The Outsiders* stands apart.

As I will illustrate in the forthcoming chapters, the film's exceptionality within the canon of youth cinema stems from the remarkable coalescence of author, director, actors, narrative, and theme.

For this reason and many more, *The Outsiders* endures – both for those of us who, almost 40 years ago, watched its premiere with wide eyes and for those who have only recently discovered what it means to stay gold.

Notes

1 In the years following the movie's release, Coppola 'received letters from kids praising the movie, but wondering why more of their favorite book wasn't in it' (Coyle 2005). His reason for returning to the film more than two decades after its debut rested solely on having to face an audience of teenagers and explain his choices: 'I think for me, the showdown was when my granddaughter's class asked me to come and show the film and I was embarrassed to show the normal version [...] So I cobbled together a version of the whole movie, the whole novel, and I remember looking at it and wondering, "Why did I ever cut this down?"' (quoted in Coyle 2005). Here, Coppola demonstrates both his thoughtful consideration of family and his desire to satisfy young people, points that I further highlight in Chapter 2.

2 Rankings of the 1982 films: #6, #20, and #30 respectively; rankings of the 1983 films: #8 and #23 respectively.

1 The Life and Legacy of S.E. Hinton's Novel

When *The Outsiders* hit theaters in March 1983, it was already a known quantity to many of its U.S. viewers. Indeed, Hinton's novel had been well-established as a Young Adult (YA) classic by the time production on the movie had been green-lighted, so unlike most of youth films of the era, Coppola's film came in part with a built-in audience that already knew its narrative well, if not by heart. What prompted Coppola to direct an adaptation of a book that at the time was almost 15 years old? As diehard fans of the film know, it all started with a letter from Jo Ellen Misakian, a librarian at Lone Star Elementary School in Fresno, California. Her middle-school students – especially the boys, who were often resistant to reading – loved Hinton's novel, and they wanted to see it realized as a film. In March 1980, she wrote a letter to Coppola on behalf of her students, asking him to consider reading the book and making it into a film. At the end of the letter, she included a petition signed by over 100 seventh- and eighth-graders in support of the request.

Misakian sent the letter to Coppola's New York studio, which by sheer luck turned out to be exactly the place for it to be seen: the studio where a letter like hers would not be buried among the thousands of other letters sent to Coppola in Los Angeles. 'It was lucky for the kids that we were in New York when it was sent over,' said Fred Roos, Coppola's producer. 'Francis doesn't get much mail in New York, so he read the letter' (quoted in Harmetz 1983). Intrigued, Coppola told Roos to read the book if he thought it might have potential. Roos resisted at first – 'The jacket was so tacky. It looked like the book was privately printed by some religious organization,' he said – but eventually he did and came to a single conclusion: 'I thought it was a movie' (ibid.). Coppola read the book a few months later and agreed. After striking a very modest deal with Hinton, filming began, and as I will discuss in the next chapter, Coppola and Hinton worked side by

DOI: 10.4324/9781003228783-2

side in creating a production experience that centered on the emotional lives of both the characters and the actors who played them. But what made the film possible at all was the already-established, loyal fan base of Hinton's novel – a fan base exemplified by the students at Lone Star School. In 1980, their love of the novel was shared by millions of other readers in the United States. And those readers then knew, as they do now, that *The Outsiders* transforms those who enter the pages of the novel. Without S.E. Hinton, Coppola's film would not exist.

It is not a stretch to say that without S.E. Hinton, the genre of YA literature as we know it would not exist, either. Author Richard Peck, who wrote his first YA novel *Don't Look and It Won't Hurt* in 1972 and followed with 40 books more over the course of his career, called Hinton 'the mother of us all' (1993: 19) and described *The Outsiders* as 'a blazing, unlikely melodrama that became one of the most widely read novels in the history of print and ignited a new tradition of American books that look at the world through the eyes of the young' (20). To be sure, the through line from *The Outsiders* to contemporary YA best sellers such as John Green's *The Fault in Our Stars* (2012) and Angie Thomas's *The Hate U Give* (2017) – novels that deal with illness, death, and racism – is clear. As journalist Margaret Eby writes in 'Why *The Outsiders* Still Matters,' 'the most abiding lesson that Hinton taught authors about writing for teenagers is that they didn't need to water down their prose to relate to a younger audience' (2017). No book-length study of Coppola's *The Outsiders* can proceed, then, without first recognizing and analyzing the source material from which it sprang – in this case, material that was truly groundbreaking in terms of genre and theme. In this chapter, I will offer an overview of the publication, reception, and impact of Hinton's novel, followed by an analysis of one of the central themes of the novel: male intimacy and love. I argue that Hinton's rendering of affection through both language and touch is one of the keys to the novel's lasting success.

The Book That Started It All

The story of the novel's conception, the author's writing process, and the book's publication are now all but apocryphal among fans of Hinton's work. Hinton, a student at Will Rogers High School in Tulsa, Oklahoma in the mid-1960s, was an outsider herself, self-described as 'a little eccentric' who was 'friends with greasers, Socs, artsy-craftsies. I could talk to all of them because I wasn't any of them' (quoted in Daly 1989: 2). Frustrated by the emphasis on social status among her peers and distressed by the violence she witnessed both at Will Rogers and in

Tulsa, Hinton set out to write a book that reflected the life she knew, a life that included class stratification, gang conflict, and violence. In various interviews, Hinton has shared that when she was a teen, one of her friends was beat up at school, and 'a real boy like Dallas Winston was shot and killed by the police' (4); these experiences became the inspiration for *The Outsiders*. Most important to her was that her story did *not* portray teenagers as they had long been imagined in literature: in her words, as a 'carefree group' whose main concern was dating. In 'Teen-Agers are For Real,' an article she wrote for the *New York Times Book Review* in 1967, Hinton laid bare her attitude toward these stories. 'The world is changing, yet the authors of books for teen-agers are still 15 years behind the times.' Hinton urged writers to embrace a realism that they had long shied away from. 'Teen-agers should not be written down to,' Hinton said firmly and bluntly. 'The teen-age years are a bad time' (1967b: 27, 29).

That 'bad time' – what she experienced and witnessed at Will Rogers – became the foundation for *The Outsiders*, a manuscript she wrote during her junior year of high school (and, as Hinton herself likes to note, at the same time that she was earning a grade of D in her creative writing class). Two years later, when she was a freshman at the University of Tulsa, 'she showed the completed manuscript for *The Outsiders* to a fellow student whose mother was an author,' and from there it passed through the hands of another writer, then a literary agent, and finally Viking Press, the second publisher to whom it was sent and ultimately sold (Howard 2001: 12). Rather than using her actual first name – Susie – the publishers chose a 'more genderless author name' so as not to scare away potential male readers (Jones 2012: 20). And though initially marketed to an adult audience, in a short time *The Outsiders* became a hit among young readers. Within a year of the novel's publication, Hinton was receiving letters from other teens expressing 'fervent gratitude that someone had written a book about the way things really were' (Sutherland 1968: 34). As Stephanie Zacharek writes in the *New York Times* about the novel on its 40th anniversary, when it was published *The Outsiders* 'cut to the heart of teenage anxiety and confusion as no other book had' (2007).[1]

Hinton biographer Jay Daly asserts that 'the world of young adult writing and publishing has never been the same' since the publication of *The Outsiders* (1989: Preface). This claim cannot be overstated. Thematically and stylistically, *The Outsiders* marked a significant departure in what was considered an 'appropriate' novel for and about teenagers. In her aforementioned essay in the *New York Times*, a young Hinton contended that

> [t]hose [teens] who are not ready for adult novels can easily have their love of reading killed by the inane junk lining the teen age shelf in the library. Parents complain of their children's lack of enthusiasm, but if they had to read a "Jeri Doe, Girl Reporter" series, they'd turn off, too.
>
> (1967b: 29)

Her suggestion to readers and writers alike: write about the *actual* lived experience of young people. As Hinton succinctly and pointedly stated, '[t]een-agers today want to read about teen-agers today' (26). Rather than reflecting contemporary teen concerns, however, authors hoping to engage young readers instead wrote about idealized romance or told tales of 'a-horse-and-the-girl-who-loved-it' (27). Other critics of the teenage literary landscape of the late 1960s were equally reproving. For example, in a 1968 essay entitled 'An End to Nostalgia,' children's writer Maia Wojciechowska lamented how authors of novels for teens 'write tepid little stories of high school proms, broken and amended friendships, phony-sounding conflicts between parents and children, and boring accounts of what they consider "problems" [...] The gulf between the real child of today and his fictional counterpart must be bridged' (1968: 13). Hinton was the author who bridged that gulf.[2]

When the reviews came in for *The Outsiders*, they recognized that Hinton's book was inaugurating a significant shift in the genre. Thomas Fleming, writing in the *New York Times Book Review*, stated that Hinton 'has produced a book alive with the fresh dialogue of her contemporaries, and has wound around it a story that captures, in vivid patches at least, a rather unnerving slice of teen-age America' (1967: 10). Similarly, in *School Library Journal*, Lillian N. Gerhardt declared that '[i]t is rare-to-unique among juvenile books (where even the non-fiction concentrates on positive aspects of American life and ignores its underside) to find a novel confronting the class hostilities which have intensified since the Depression'; she praised *The Outsiders* for 'tell[ing] how it looks and feels from the wrong side of the tracks' (1967: 64-5). Nat Hentoff, writing for *Wilson Library Bulletin*, claimed that 'if a book is relevant to [teenagers'] concerns, not didactically, but in creating textures of experiences which teenagers can recognize as germane to their own, it can merit their attention' (1968: 263). Hentoff identified *The Outsiders* as such a book. Other critics praised the novel for its honesty and humanity. Zena Sutherland, in *Saturday Review*, described *The Outsiders* as 'written with distinctive style by a teen-ager who is sensitive, honest, and observant' (1967: 59). In *Children's Book News,* Aidan Chambers concurred, noting how the novel had 'remarkably interesting qualities [...] [t]he story has humour, passion, tenderness, intelligence, action a-plenty and, best of all, compassion' (1970: 280). Collectively, these critics recognized how *The Outsiders* was bound to change the literary world and pave the way for a new genre – a genre that, years later, is now flourishing globally (Jensen 2020).

Certainly not all of the reviews for Hinton's novel saw it as a revolutionary publication; 'those with reservations mostly found the book erred on the side of over-sentimentality and clichéd writing' (Jones 2012: 20). Some critics who recommended and praised the novel at the same time identified its sentimentality, its 'factitious' plot (a word used by both Hentoff and the *Times Literary Supplement*), or the 'over-didacticism of its first person narrative' (Chambers 1970: 280) as a strike against it. The most famous negative review appeared in *Kirkus Review*, where the sardonic appraisal of the book concludes with the now-ironic line: 'You can believe a teen-ager wrote it but you can bet teen-agers won't believe what it says' ('Review of *The Outsiders*' 1967: 507). Obviously, that reviewer was dead wrong. Within a few years of its publication, *The Outsiders* not only had gained a following of teen readers in the United States but also had changed the landscape of the Anglo-American publishing world. Unexpectedly, and despite its perceived sentimentality – or perhaps because of it – *The Outsiders* opened a world of possibility for writers of teen fiction *and* for readers of it.

Literary critic Caren J. Town expounds upon the significance of *The Outsiders*, observing that 'most critics and historians of the genre agree that *The Outsiders'* publication was a landmark event' (2014: 15). Hinton's novel ushered in an era of 'New Realism' of literature for teenagers as well as kick-started, if not created, the genre of YA fiction.[3] Because 'the publishing industry's assumptions about the interests and maturity level of teen readers had never allowed for the degree of sobering realism found in *The Outsiders*' (Howard 2001: 8), the impact of Hinton's novel, as well as its fast-growing popularity, came as a surprise to both Hinton and the industry. The publisher, Viking Press, initially 'marketed *The Outsiders* as an adult title and with little fanfare' (27) – and thus, as Hinton herself noted, it almost 'died on the vine being sold as a drugstore paperback' (quoted in Michaud 2014). But then, according to Hinton, Viking 'noticed that in one area it was selling very well. Teachers were using it in classes. All of a sudden, they realized that there was a separate market for young adults' (ibid.). In the 50-year wake of *The Outsiders*, this market has thrived.

While *The Outsiders* is often identified as having established a 'New Realism' in YA (if not establishing the genre of YA literature itself), over the years the question of its realism has been a subject of debate. How realistic is it, for example, for gang members to read *Gone with the Wind* and memorize Robert Frost poems? In his important study *Young Adult Literature: From Romance to Realism*, Michael Cart acknowledges Hinton's 'significant place in the evolution of young adult literature' but asserts that *The Outsiders* is a 'hybrid' genre, 'part realistic fiction and part romantic fantasy' (2010: 27), pointing specifically to the idealized characters and sentimental theme of maintaining one's innocence and 'staying gold.' In her book *Youth Gangs in Literature*, Claudia Durst Johnson likewise challenges the realism of *The Outsiders*, proclaiming that '[t]he camaraderie of gang members [in the novel] creates an idealistic picture that gains the reader's admiration, but it ignores the truth that throughout history the chief victims of gangs are their own members.' She ultimately claims that '[t]he strength of the novel is not its realism, but rather its idealism' (2004: 122). Other literary critics are more unforgiving in their analyses. David Rees, in his blistering essay 'Macho Man, American Style,' claims that '[t]here is nothing here for the adult; maybe because S. E. Hinton fails to convince the reader of the reality of her world' (1984: 128). Describing the letter that a dying Johnny writes to Ponyboy, Rees proclaims, 'This isn't realism. It's fantasy, in the worst sense of the word […] The characters are either incredible or unsympathetic, the action often repetitive, the implied attitudes questionable' (134). Likewise, in her book *Reading for the Love of It*, Michele Landsberg calls the novel 'preposterous' and 'absurd' (1987: 214, 215).

While the arguments calling into question the realism of *The Outsiders* certainly make some germane points, I would also argue that they obscure why the novel has endured for as long as it has. As both reader and critic, I am less interested in the question of the degrees of realism in *The Outsiders* and more interested in further examining why the novel has resonated with so many readers over the years. The first and perhaps most obvious reason is its thoughtful treatment of social class. Literary scholar Eric L. Tribunella states that '*The Outsiders* is rather remarkable for its consciousness of class issues' (2010: 62), and he offers an insightful and complex analysis of 'the problems of social class and class inequality' in the novel (66). Similarly, Sandra Beals recognizes how 'Ponyboy provides compelling evidence for the existence and methods of systematic, class-based oppression of greasers by Socs, as well as a clear picture of how it feels to the greasers, particularly Ponyboy, to live under this oppression' (2018: 196). Many of the aforementioned reviews of the novel likewise praise Hinton's depiction of class tensions as remarkable in its honesty and accuracy. As Nat Hentoff asserts: 'Any teen-ager, no matter what some of his [sic] textbooks say, knows that this is decidedly not a classless society [...] [*The Outsiders*] explores the tenacious loyalties on both sides of the class divide' (1968: 263). The stark socioeconomic differences between the Greasers and the Socs are made explicit through Ponyboy's frank narrative style. Whether he is bitterly protesting aloud to his friends that '[i]t ain't fair that we have all the rough breaks!' (Hinton 1967a: 43) or reflecting internally that 'most grownups don't know about the battles that go on between us' (107), Ponyboy never shrinks from telling his readers the truth of his situation: he and his gang are viewed as 'white trash' by society.[4] Over the course of the novel, he begins to let go of his class resentment and see the Socs not as 'rich kids' but as people: 'Things were rough all over, but it was better that way. That way you could tell the other guy was human too' (118). At the same time, he understands the importance of telling both his own story and the stories of his Greaser friends so that people 'wouldn't be so quick to judge a boy by the amount of hair oil he wore' (179). As Hentoff rightly notes, *The Outsiders* appeals to 'heterogeneous sections of the young because it stimulates their own feelings and questionings about class and differing life-styles' (1968: 263).[5]

The second reason for the novel's lasting impact is what Thomas Reed Whissen calls its 'unmistakable authenticity' (1992: 184). This authenticity is exemplified in Ponyboy's narrative voice but also in the interpersonal relationships that populate the novel: relationships primarily of male camaraderie and intimacy. For as tough as the boys are, they feel deeply, and I would argue that the depth of their feeling has contributed to the lasting impact of Hinton's novel and the abiding love that readers across generations feel for Ponyboy and the gang. In the second half of this chapter, I discuss three fundamental characteristics of the novel: Ponyboy's narration; the emotional depth of the characters and the care they evince for each other; and the numerous references to crying, which underscore the boys' youth and vulnerability. While some critics point to these aspects of the novel as evidence of its sentimentality and lack of realism, I view them as the very reason that the novel's readership has endured over so many decades: because Hinton allows us to see the heart that lies behind the tough veneer of the boys; because it is 'a book pulsing with teenage boys whose primary value is friendship' (Dunham 2018).

Authenticity, Vulnerability, and Brotherhood

I was 12 years old when I first read *The Outsiders*: an adolescent myself like Ponyboy, trying to make sense of the world. Up until that point, the only other book I had read with a first-person narrator whose experience resonated with my own was Judy Blume's *Are You There, God? It's Me, Margaret* (1970). But Blume's novel spoke specifically to my experiences of being an adolescent girl: hitting puberty and dealing with the concomitant changes in my body and weird feelings for boys, those creatures who only one year earlier had been, in my mind, icky and dumb. *The Outsiders* was different. I can still remember the night I read it. Earlier in the day, my oldest sister Lisa had picked up a copy of it from a thrift store and handed it to me, saying, 'I think you'd like this book.' I was sitting on my bed looking at the tattered paperback cover – a red background with a group of mod-looking guys, two of them wearing sunglasses – wondering what this book was about and whether I should even open it up. I did, and upon reading the iconic first line – 'When I stepped out into the bright sunlight from the darkness of the movie house, I had only two things on my mind: Paul Newman and a ride home' – I was hooked. Several hours later, when the novel concluded with that same line, a sense of awe, satisfaction, and love washed over me. In the years that followed, I reread *The Outsiders* more than any other book on my shelf or in the library. And more than any other book in my early life, it made me love reading.

It seems unlikely that a 12-year-old white, middle-class, Catholic school girl from suburbia would find so much in *The Outsiders* to identify with as a reader, but the fact is, I did. I identified with Ponyboy's voice and writing; with his love of poetry; with his affection for his friends; and most of all, with his attempt to make sense of the world through words. Whissen observes that '[t]he story that Ponyboy tells is a boy's story, and boys continue to identify with its narrator and his buddies. But the story also holds a powerful fascination for girls who can wax ecstatic about the way this book is their voice' (1992: 186). I was and still am one of those girls. Even as a teen, I was attuned to one of the key components of the novel's strength: its narrative voice.[6] Described by Stephanie Zacharek as the novel's 'confused but eminently likable narrator' (2007), Ponyboy is not only the voice of the story but the moral center of it as well. He is also young enough not to be a young man in the way that Dally is, i.e., threatening or, in Cherry's words, 'dirty.' In this way, his gender identity is, as June Pulliam puts it, 'ambiguous' (2012: 83) – and as such, this 'boy's story' could just as accurately be described as an *adolescent's* story.[7] The fact that 'Pony is not cool' and that 'his emotions are constantly gaining control over his thought process' opens up further identificatory possibilities for readers (Wistisen 2021: 206). Whether he is sharing how he copes with his pain – 'I lie to myself all the time. But I never believe me' (Hinton 1967a: 18) – or how he shamefully realizes that he and Darry are 'play[ing] tug of war' with Soda's feelings (175), Ponyboy's voice always seems honest and authentic. By the end of the novel, Ponyboy 'emerges from pain with a message of encouragement' (Whissen 1992: 189); his resolve in the face of adversity is admirable, a model for young readers who themselves might be struggling with adolescent life.

The adult reader I am now is attuned even more deeply to one of the novel's most dominant themes as expressed through Ponyboy's narration: love as expressed through care and touch. In a 1970 review of the novel, the *Times Literary Supplement* noted that the most significant aspect of the novel is its emphasis on 'the nature of gang loyalty and family affection in a world which is hostile to Greasers' ('Review of *The Outsiders*' 1970: 1258). Teacher and critic Ellen A. Seay concurs, observing that the Greasers 'have a brotherhood, a unity amongst their own for which they are willing to fight. They take care of and are concerned about each other' (2012: 98). While Ponyboy is by far the most adept at expressing his emotions – he is, after all, our narrator, and as such readers are privy to them as they are with no other characters – the other gang members likewise evince an emotional depth that binds them to each other and allows them to support and even parent one another. This parenting is most obvious in Darry, of course, who has had to assume the role of guardian in the wake of the elder Curtis's deaths, but it is also notable in three other characters: Sodapop, Dally, and Johnny. Sodapop, about whom Ponyboy says he 'love[s] […] more than I've ever loved anyone' (Hinton 1967a: 2), functions as both protective, loving brother and gentle mother-substitute for Ponyboy. He shares a bed with Ponyboy, and when they sleep together, he often 'threw one arm across my neck' (17). He also promises to wait to marry his girlfriend, Sandy, until after Ponyboy has graduated from high school (18). After Ponyboy's been jumped by the Greasers, Soda 'put his hand on my shoulder' and reassured Ponyboy, 'They ain't gonna hurt you no more' (8). In the wake of the rumble, Soda 'stroked my hair' (155), comforting him like a mother might. Soda takes on a maternal role in relation to the gang, too. After the rumble, 'Steve lay doubled up and groaning about ten feet from me […] Sodapop was beside him, talking in a low steady voice' (145). Later, when

Dally is gunned down by police, 'Steve stumbled forward with a sob, but Soda caught him by the shoulders' (154). Undeniably, 'these tough gang members are extremely sensitive, demonstrative, and emotive' (Abate 2017: 54), and among the gang, Soda stands out as the most tender, offering emotional and physical comfort to his brother and his friends.

Dally seems an unlikely candidate for taking on a parental role vis-à-vis the other characters – after all, he himself has been in trouble with the law since the age of ten – but toward the two youngest members of the gang, Johnny and Ponyboy, Dally shares his street smarts in order to keep them safe and his clothes to keep them warm. After Johnny kills Bob, Dally gives them a plan, money, and a gun. He instructs them on how to act when they arrive at Windrixville and how to stay safe. His care of them is embodied in the leather jacket his gives to Ponyboy. Ponyboy describes how without hesitation, Dally 'handed me his worn brown leather jacket with the yellow sheep's-wool lining. "It'll get cold where you're going, but you can't risk being loaded down with blankets"' (Hinton 1967a: 61). While running away on the train to Windrixville, Ponyboy says that 'I was thankful for Dally's jacket. It was too big, but it was warm' (62). After saving children from the burning church, Ponyboy is told that the same jacket 'saved you from a bad burning, maybe saved your life' (94). Dally's jacket emblematizes his 'fiercely loyal' character (Howard 2001: 46) and his care of the boys, protecting the youngest gang member from harm. When Johnny reveals that he wants to turn himself in to the cops, Dally says 'in a pleading, high voice, using a tone I had never heard from him before, "Johnny, I ain't mad at you. I just don't want you to get hurt. You don't know what a few months in jail can do to you"' (Hinton 1967a: 89). He saves Johnny from the burning church (93) and dies hours after Johnny, having given up on life without his friend. As *Beacham's Guide to Literature for Young Adults* observes, Dally 'seldom expresses his emotions. The only person whom he allows himself tender feelings for is Johnny, who represents all of the innocence and humanity that Dally himself has lost' (McCormick 1989: 1009). In parenting both Ponyboy and Johnny, Dally transcends the label of 'hood' placed upon him by society at large.

Lastly, there is Johnny Cade, arguably the emotional center and the hero of the book. Despite, or perhaps because of, Johnny's status as the most vulnerable member of the gang – Ponyboy describes him as a 'little dark puppy that has been kicked too many times' (Hinton 1967a: 11) – he is the most beloved member of the group, 'the gang's pet, everyone's kid brother' (12). Adopted and taken under the wings of the rest of the gang, Johnny finds a place of protection in their care; as Ponyboy reveals, '[i]f it hadn't been for the gang, Johnny would never have known what love and affection are' (ibid.). And yet, despite his own experiences of trauma, Johnny provides love and affection to his fellow gang members. After his fight with Darry, Ponyboy goes straight to Johnny, and together the two of them 'ran for several blocks until we were out of breath. Then we walked. I was crying by then. I finally just sat down on the curb and cried, burying my face in my hands. Johnny sat down beside me, one hand on my shoulder. "Easy, Ponyboy," he said softly, "we'll be okay"' (51). Later, when he and Ponyboy are running away on the train, Ponyboy describes how he 'stretched out and used Johnny's legs as a pillow' (62), as a child might do with their parent. Similarly, when they are days into their exile in Windrixville, Johnny comforts a distraught Ponyboy: 'Don't cry, Pony, we'll be okay. Don't cry [...] (75). Ponyboy then 'leaned against him and bawled until I went to sleep' (ibid.). Though he comes from a physically and verbally abusive household, Johnny rejects such behavior for himself. Rather, he parents and nurtures Ponyboy, providing him with comfort and care through physical touch and verbal reassurance. As Ponyboy reflects after Johnny's death, he 'was something more than a buddy to all of us. I guess he had listened to more beefs and more problems from more people than any of us. A guy that'll really listen to you, listen and care about what you're saying, is something rare' (178).

Finally, there is the most obvious way in which the boys' vulnerability presents itself in this story: through tears. The role and frequency of crying in *The Outsiders* is an issue that critics have pointed to as dual proof of the book's immature sentimentality and lack of realism (or, in one instance, as proof of the writer's sex[8]). More recent analyses of the novel, however, identify it as a strength rather than a detriment. Journalist Hayley Krischer comments that '[w]hat may be most remarkable about the greasers is their ability to show great affection and emotion despite the masculine-dominated cultural norms of the 1960s' (2017). I agree, and as an adult reader of the novel, I see this even more clearly. At least 15 times throughout the novel, Ponyboy references crying, bawling, or being on the verge of tears. Most of the time, Ponyboy himself is crying or trying not to cry. He cries after he's jumped by the Socs (Hinton 1967a: 8); days into his exile with Johnny in Windrixville (73); during a conversation with Johnny about how scared they are (74); and after chasing Soda through the park and promising not to fight with Darry anymore (176). He also holds back tears in several scenes, including when he first arrives at the hospital: 'I was trembling. A pain was growing in my throat and I wanted to cry, but greasers don't cry in front of strangers. Some of us never cry at all. Like Dally and Two-Bit and Tim Shepard – they forgot how at an early age' (102-3). He does the same when visiting Johnny at the hospital: 'Don't start crying, I commanded myself, don't start crying, you'll scare Johnny' (121). He also mentions moments when other characters cry, including Johnny (33, 74), Soda (40, 176), Darry (98), Two-Bit (123), and Cherry (129, 168). The motif of tears reminds readers that Ponyboy is still a kid, a boy who just turned 14 and who is not savvy enough to make his own way in the world or fully manage his emotions. It also reminds readers that *all* of the Greasers – even the tough ones like Dally – are still boys, still young and vulnerable.

After meeting Soc Cherry at the drive-in and walking home with her after the movie, she and Ponyboy have a conversation about what separates them. Ponyboy says that 'maybe it was money' (Hinton 1967a: 38). Cherry responds that money is part of the difference, but that the central distinction is that 'greasers have a different set of values. You're more emotional. We're sophisticated – cool to the point of not feeling anything.' Ponyboy ponders this observation and ultimately agrees with Cherry, responding, 'That's why we're separated [...]. It's not money, it's feeling – you don't feel anything and we feel too violently' (38). It is noteworthy that Ponyboy uses the word 'violently' here to describe emotion, since the violence is one of the reasons *The Outsiders* has appeared on banned books lists over the past 50 years ('Banned Books ...' 2011). And certainly, as Karen Coats suggests, it is important to analyze 'the role of physical violence in the complex rhetoric of loyalty, masculinity, and fraternal love that comprises coming of age for Ponyboy' (2011: 317).[9] But I would argue that it is equally important to explore the role of feeling among the boys in that complex rhetoric. In its representation of affection between Ponyboy and his friends and its depiction of the Greasers as a 'surrogate family' for each other (Inderbitzin 2003: 357), *The Outsiders* offers a model of male intimacy and fraternal love that is extraordinary. Indeed, '[t]he emotional community of the greasers provides the boys with the tenderness missing from their relationships with their parents. The community thus creates space for actions of love and vulnerability, as well as enabling the formation of a more sensitive masculine identity' (Wistisen 2021: 208).

Conclusion

The effectiveness with which these admirable characters and these intense feelings, both personal and familial, get translated into the film adaptation of the novel are the purview of the next two chapters. Coppola's realization of Hinton's novel captures all of these emotions, and more. It strays very little from the story itself, and if anything, it imagines the intimacy among the Greasers in ways that are tender and touching. As I explore in the next chapter, the sense of brotherhood evinced in the novel and captured in the film in fact preceded it: it began with the casting call itself and continued throughout the filming process, wherein Coppola and Hinton functioned as parental figures for the young men bringing the characters to life.

Notes

1 For an excellent discussion of the literary and cultural influences on Hinton, see Dale Peck, '*The Outsiders*: 40 Years Later' (2007).

2 There is very little information on the international reach or impact of Hinton's book. Indeed, most research on the novel assumes a U.S. readership, which makes sense given the novel's author and primary reading audience. Recently, however, *The Outsiders* appeared on the BBC Arts's list of 100 'most inspiring' novels ('100 "Most Inspiring" Novels [...]' 2019), a list dominated by British authors. And, as I note in Chapter 5, *The Outsiders* has been translated into over 30 languages (Krischer 2017), including Spanish, French, German, Russian, Japanese, Turkish, Korean, and most recently, Chinese. The range of languages included herein suggests a global readership, even if only on a small scale.

3 The question of the 'origin' of the YA adult novel is one taken up by many scholars of the genre. In his essay 'From Insider to Outsiders: The Evolution of Young Adult Literature' (2001), Michael Cart offers a succinct summary of the issue:

> Students of the history of young adult literature will know that the first golden age came very early in the life of this still relatively new genre, since YA literature – the genre formerly known as 'realistic fiction for teens' – didn't appear until 1967 with the publication of S.E. Hinton's *The Outsiders* and Robert Lipsyte's *The Contender*. However, a case could be made that the first young adult novel was actually Maureen Daly's *Seventeenth Summer*, published in 1942, about the same time that America began recognizing the teenage years as a separate part of the life cycle.
>
> (2001: 96)

In her essay '*The Outsiders,* Fat Freddy, and Me,' Patty Campbell (2003) also cites Lipsyte's novel as a landmark YA text, along with Paul Zindel's *The Pigman* (1968) and Ann Head's *Mr. and Mrs. Bo Jo Jones* (1967). Both Cart and Campbell are critical of Hinton's novel – Campbell calls it 'melodramatic and crudely written' (2003: 180) – but recognize its importance in the YA canon.

4 That the Greasers are called 'white trash' underscores both the class and the racial dynamics of their world. Living in what was essentially a still-segregated Tulsa in the 1960s, the Greasers and Socs interact primarily with white people like themselves, but the Greasers are reminded of their lower class status by this pejorative, which at once distinguishes them from 'good' white people and people of color. These class and racial dynamics are evident, too, in Johnny's idealization of the 'gallant' soldiers in *Gone With the Wind*. As Claudia Durst Johnson notes, 'Johnny is transfixed by the gallantry of nineteenth-century southern gentlemen, ignoring the slavery, class snobbery, and meaningless violence that characterized them' (2004: 122). Johnny's romanticizing of southern gallantry, absent of its racist underpinnings, perhaps is a limitation of his character and the novel, but it is also a potentially realistic rendering of a teenager who has meager educational and familial resources available to him.

5 The extent to which Ponyboy is assimilated into the individualistic, middle-class values at the expense of his authenticity and his loyalty to family and friends is a subject of ongoing debate among literary scholars. On the one hand, critics like Sandra Beals claim that '*The Outsiders* models the development of critical consciousness of classist ideology and invites readers to participate in "consciousness-raising." It does its consciousness-raising, anticlassist work through its narrative structure, by talking to multiple audiences' (2018: 197). Other readers of the novel are much more critical in their assessment of Ponyboy's relationship to middle-class values, asserting that 'the novel undermines its own purported critique of social class' and 'maintains and reproduces social order' (Wistisen 2021: 202). Most notably, in his book *Melancholia and Maturation* Eric L. Tribunella contends that '[a]fter establishing the problems associated with social class – systemic and generational inequality, alienation and malaise – the novel concludes by offering what it represents as a possible solution to that problem: Ponyboy's education and individualism' (2010: 67).

6 Over the years Hinton has been questioned about why her narrators are male. Regarding *The Outsiders* she stated the following: 'I started writing before the women's movement was in full swing, and at the time, people wouldn't have believed that girls would do the things that I was writing about. I also felt more comfortable with the male point of view – I had grown up around boys' (quoted in Erhlich 1981: 32). In another interview, she articulates how in her teenage years, the female point of view seemed too limited: 'In those days, girls were mainly concerned about getting their hair done and lining their eyes. It was such a passive society. Girls got their status from their boyfriends. They weren't interested in doing anything on their own. I didn't understand what they were talking about' (quoted in Farber 1983).

7 And, from another point of view, a heterosexual girl's story. As Michele Ann Abate observes, 'Ponyboy's descriptions of the physical appearance of the greaser gang get so lengthy and detailed that [...] they begin to suggest the write-ups in teen idol magazines such as *Tiger Beat*' (Abate 2017: 50). Abate's connection between *The Outsiders* and teen magazines parallels how the film was marketed, which I discuss in Chapter 4.

8 Per Lillian N. Gerhardt in *School Library Journal*: 'In retrospect the obvious clue [that Hinton is a female] is that maybe only a girl could broadcast,

without alibi, the soft centers of these boys and how often they do give way to tears' (1967: 65).

9 This intimacy is not without its problems. As some critics have pointed out, it is often predicated on misogyny. *Beacham's Guide to Literature for Young Adults*, for example, remarks that 'the most curious problem with *The Outsiders* is its sexism. Hinton chooses to focus almost exclusively on male characters and has little to say, let alone anything positive, about the greasers' female counterparts. […] For someone who crusades against labeling and stereotyping, Ponyboy exhibits an attitude [toward females] that does not make sense' (McCormick 1989: 1012). David Rees concurs, asserting that in Hinton's novels '[g]irls are "chicks" – not much more than status symbols – important only as possessions, along with cigarettes, liquor, cars, and the hardware used in a rumble' (1984: 127). I do not disagree with these critiques of the novel. Ponyboy's dismissal of girls – especially those in his social sphere (Hinton 1967a: 14-5) – is troubling. At the same time, it is important to remember that he is a 14-year-old boy, and for all of his insights, he is still essentially a child making sense of his world. In one of his most noteworthy reflections, he says, 'we try to be nice to the girls we see once in a while […] but we still watch a nice girl go by on a street corner and say all kinds of lousy stuff about her. Don't ask me why. I don't know why' (26). In such instances, I read his sexism as a reflection of his age, social sphere, and gender expectations. While he seemingly accepts an attitude of casual disdain for girls (excepting Cherry), he also exhibits an ability to reflect and change in ways that suggest these attitudes could shift as he becomes an adult. Such change is modeled for him by Johnny, who stands up to Dally when he is harassing Cherry (24-5). In doing so, Johnny embodies a young manhood not predicated on aggression or disrespect toward females.

2 Francis Ford Coppola and *The Outsiders*

Famous Director Turned Camp Counselor

It was the early 1980s, and things were not looking good for Francis Coppola.[1] His pet project, the 1982 romantic musical *One from the Heart*, had ballooned significantly over budget, starting at a modest \$2 million but ultimately costing more than ten times that amount, an enormous \$27 million (Phillips 2004: 197). Due to explosive conflicts between Coppola and the brass at Paramount, its distribution ping-ponged from studio to studio, eventually landing, albeit uneasily, at Columbia Pictures. In an attempt to garner audience feedback on the film and to counter the negative press about its troubled production, Coppola scheduled an extravagant preview at Radio City Music Hall in January 1982. His plan backfired. The film was poorly received, and in the face of scathing reviews and a U.S. box-office return that was dismal – it earned less than \$1 million during its release – things went from bad to worse. Due to the enormous costs of the movie, Coppola was swimming in debt, and the production company he had co-founded with George Lucas in 1969, American Zoetrope, was facing its demise. In the wake of the critical, commercial, and financial disaster of *One from the Heart,* Coppola retreated to Tulsa, Oklahoma, to pursue a project that was at once financially viable and personally restorative. The name of that project was *The Outsiders* (Schumacher 1999: 305-16). As Coppola himself explained:

> I escaped with a lot of young people to Tulsa and didn't have to deal with the sophisticates. I had been a camp counselor when I was younger, and I always got along very well with kids. I like being with kids rather than adults, so it turned into a way for me to soothe my heartache over the terrible rejection at that point.
>
> (quoted in Thomson and Gray 1983: 64)

DOI: 10.4324/9781003228783-3

Two aspects of this reflection from Coppola are noteworthy. The first is the way in which he describes *The Outsiders* as a project that could 'soothe [his] heartache' over the critical and commercial failure of *One from the Heart*. In doing so, Coppola highlights how from the outset, *The Outsiders* was a project in which he had an emotional investment, and he brought this affective energy to bear on the experience of making the film. The second is his claim he 'like[s] being with kids rather than adults.' His rejection of the 'sophisticates' of Hollywood over the experiences and instincts of young people in fact characterizes every aspect of the production of *The Outsiders*. To be sure, part of what situates the film within the larger genre of youth cinema is not only its narrative content and formal characteristics – which I will discuss in the next chapter – but also the production values that informed the making of the film. This chapter explores and analyzes how Coppola cultivated and formed 'a kind of mutual admiration society' with the cast (Schumacher 1999: 323), the result being a film that is decidedly different both from others in his oeuvre and from the teen movies hitting the theaters in the early 1980s. At every turn, Coppola centered and appreciated the youthfulness of his cast, and in doing so, he created new possibilities for cinema to capture, create, and highlight youth culture.

The Troubled – and Charmed – Path to *The Outsiders*

The opportunity to direct *The Outsiders* came at just the right time for Coppola. Ten years earlier, he was at the start of what would be a remarkable directorial run in the 1970s, bookended by the two films for which he is best known, an adaptation of Mario Puzo's story of the mob and family ties, *The Godfather* (1972), and the epic Vietnam film *Apocalypse Now* (1979). In between those two movies came *The Godfather Part II* (1974) and Coppola's first pet project, the critically acclaimed but commercially unsuccessful *The Conversation* (1974). Coppola's legacy as an auteur and continued success in the new decade of the 1980s seemed indisputable. Then along came his post-*Apocalypse Now* creation, a marked departure from his films of the 1970s: *One from the Heart* (1982). The story behind *One from the Heart* is one of Hollywood lore, a tale of excess and ego and miscalculations of the greatest sort. But without *One from the Heart*, it is likely Coppola never would have taken on *The Outsiders*, so some brief background on the debacle of the former film is worth noting.

One of the best accounts of *One from the Heart* appears in Lillian Ross's well-known feature article 'Some Figures on a Fantasy: Francis Coppola,' published in the *New Yorker* in November 1982. In it, Ross profiles Coppola, whom she calls an 'unpretentious man' who 'follows his feelings together with his ideas in creating his work' (2004: 64), and she details the long road to the creation – and ultimate failure – of *One from the Heart*.

Imagined by Coppola as 'a new kind of old-fashioned romance,' the film 'is the story of an unmarried couple, Frannie and Hank, who have been living together in a small house in Las Vegas for five years and are dissatisfied with each other' (74). They each dream about lives different from their mundane routines, and their dreams are shot in fantastic landscapes across Las Vegas. Most notable about these shots, however, is that none of them actually takes place on location. Rather, Coppola's commitment to creating a 'theatrical' style meant that rather than shooting in Las Vegas, 'he created his own, stylized version of Las Vegas at Zoetrope Studios' – a task that required the work of 'more than two hundred carpenters and other craftsmen' (ibid.) and thus an enormous amount of money. Both in spite of and because of Coppola's self-proclaimed desire to 'tell this simple story in a fantasy way' (ibid.), the film took almost two years to make. In that time, it spiraled out of control and consumed Coppola's life, finances, and reputation.

Ross's article attends to many fascinating details of the *One from the Heart* saga, including Coppola's trailblazing use of 'electronic cinema' in the making of the movie; the director's frustration with critics and the press; the studio's frantic attempt to manage and adjust audience expectations about the film via constant revisions to its marketing strategy; and finally, the lingering question of Coppola's reputation as a director following the movie's failure. It concludes poignantly with Coppola ruminating on the lessons he learned from the entire experience. Stung by the critical panning of a film into which he had poured his own heart and by the widespread dismissal of his attempt at cinematic creativity and innovation, Coppola reflected: 'The *most* important single thing I've learned [...] is to play everything closer to the vest from now on' (quoted in Ross 2004: 102, italics in original). Contemplating his movie and his hope and dreams for Zoetrope, Coppola said, 'I doubt whether many people understood the depth of my feelings on this subject. I have no doubt that I have the energy and resourcefulness to keep going with the studio. But sometimes I wonder whether it's worth it in such a cynical and frightening world' (quoted in Ross 2004: 104). In the wake of *One from the Heart*, Coppola's uncertainty and tempered optimism make sense. They also are crucial to understanding the attitude with which he took on *The Outsiders* as his next project.

At the same time that Coppola was pouring his heart (and money) into *One from the Heart*, another impassioned individual was determined to have a collective vision realized. That individual, mentioned briefly in Chapter 1, was Jo Ellen Misakian, the librarian at Lone Star Elementary in Fresno, California. On 21 March 1980, Misakian wrote the letter to Coppola asking him to consider making one of the students' most beloved books, S.E. Hinton's *The Outsiders*, into a film (see Figure 2.1).

SANGER UNIFIED SCHOOL DISTRICT

1905 W. SEVENTH STREET • SANGER, CALIFORNIA 93657 • PHONE 875-6521 or 237-3171

DR. J. DONALD DOROUGH
SUPERINTENDENT

ROY T. ARGLEBEN
ASST SUPT INSTR

DR. LEEDS R. LACY, JR.
ASST SUPT PERSONNEL

MICHAEL M. LINDEMANN
BUSINESS MANAGER

Lone Star School Library
2617 South Fowler Avenue
Fresno, California 93725
March 21, 1980

Mr. Francis Ford Coppola
1 Gulf and Western Plaza
New York, N. Y. 10023

Dear Mr. Copolla:

I am writing to you on behalf of the students and faculty of Lone Star School. We hope you will take the time to consider our request.

We are all so impressed with the book, THE OUTSIDERS by S. E. Hinton, that a petition has been circulated asking that it be made into a movie. We have chosen you to send it to. In hopes that you might also see the possibilities of the movie we have enclosed a copy of the book.

Lone Star is a small school in Fresno County. We have a student body of 324 students. It is a kindergarten through eighth grade school. I feel our students are representative of the youth of America. Everyone who has read the book, regardless of ethnic or economical background, has enthusiastically endorsed this project. This plea comes from our seventh and eighth grade students.

We feel certain that if you will read the book you will agree with us.

Thank you for your time.

Sincerely yours,

Jo Ellen Misakian

Jo Ellen Misakian
(Mrs. John Misakian)
Librarian Aide

SANGER—WHERE EDUCATION IS A WAY OF LIFE

Figure 2.1 Librarian Jo Ellen Misakian's letter to Coppola requesting that he make Hinton's *The Outsiders* into a film (Image courtesy of Jo Ellen Misakian)

'We are all so impressed with the book,' Misakian writes, 'that a petition has been circulated asking that it be made into a movie. We have chosen you to send it to.' She concludes the letter: 'We feel certain that if you read the book you will agree with us.' The story of Misakian's letter is 'a fairy tale that might itself have made one of the heartwarming movies Hollywood used to churn out in an innocent and less expensive era' (Harmetz 1983).

As Misakian herself noted, 'There were so many miracles associated with this story' (2021). With a librarian's keen sleuthing skills, Misakian inquired with several sources about to whom she should send her letter. She was advised to start with Hinton and did so, but Hinton did not respond, so Misakian tried another route. Having read a positive review of *The Black Stallion* (Ballard, 1979), a film produced by Coppola, Misakian decided to reach out to him next. She found the address for his office in New York City and sent him the petition and a copy of the novel. There, it found its way onto Coppola's desk and into his hands; he read the letter and told his producer, Fred Roos, 'Look at that cute letter. I bet kids have a good idea of what should be a movie. Check it out, Fred, if you want to' (quoted in Harmetz 1983). Roos reluctantly did 'check it out,' ultimately concluding it was a worthwhile project. Months later, Coppola himself read the novel and agreed. He and Roos traveled to Tulsa to meet Hinton and broker a deal. Hinton wanted a reasonable $5000 for the rights, an amount Zoetrope could not give her because they did not have the money; she agreed to 'a paltry five hundred dollars with a percentage of the profits and a part in the movie' (Bergan 1997: 65). Pre-production moved forward, with script writer Kathleen Rowell taking on the project.

The Outsiders was the perfect project to follow the disappointment of *One from the Heart* for several reasons, not the least of which was its commercial viability. Coppola biographer Michael Schumacher describes how at the time, Coppola 'had no alternative but to play the Hollywood game: Find a project with decent commercial potential; approach studio executives with hat in hand; work as a director for hire; and complete the picture on time and on budget' (1999: 316). *The Outsiders* allowed him to check all these boxes. Coppola scholar Jon Lewis likewise observes that Coppola's embrace of *The Outsiders* 'seems, even in retrospect, a calculated attempt on Coppola's part to regain his lost commercial appeal' (1995: 95). Coppola's *modus operandi* in the 1970s had generally been to direct epic films of epic lengths and with epic budgets: *The Godfather, The Godfather Part II, Apocalypse Now.* What he needed was a modest film with a modest budget and the promise of modest returns, and with a budget of $10 million dollars (99), *The Outsiders* presented him with that opportunity. As he stated after making the film, '*The Outsiders* threw up just enough money to help me at a time when I needed some big bucks' (quoted in Thomson and Gray 1983: 64).

Equally important, though, was the emotional connection that Coppola felt to the story. As noted in the earlier quote from Coppola, *The Outsiders* provided him with the opportunity to 'remove himself from the many distractions attending the various sales and foreclosures of his studio' and to escape and have fun (Lewis 1995: 100). The movie's potential spoke to him as a filmmaker: 'I wanted to take these street rats and give them heroic proportions' (quoted in Phillips 2004: 206). But it also spoke to him personally. In his study of Coppola's work, film scholar Gene D. Phillips notes that

> Coppola was convinced that *The Outsiders* was written with the authentic voice of a youngster [...] 'As I was reading the book, I realized that I wanted to make a film about young people, and about belonging,' says Coppola, 'belonging to a peer group with whom one can identify and for whom one feels real love. Even though the boys are poor and to a certain extent insignificant, the story gives them a kind of beauty and nobility.'
>
> (203)

In a more recent interview, Coppola reflects on how *The Outsiders* 'was full of emotion [...] and it showed that young people had depth of feeling for one another, and that their relationships are filled with love and affection underneath all the cynicism' (quoted in Godfrey 2021: 99). Authenticity, nobility, heroism – these are all terms that Coppola routinely used when discussing *The Outsiders*, and they make sense in light of both the film's content and the themes to which Coppola as a director is loyal. And his reiteration of how the film stood in opposition to the cynicism of Hollywood (and the larger world) is striking here. His regard of the narrative as offering something pure and authentic informed his directing of the film, as did his feeling that at the center of the story was the importance of family. 'All of the greasers were orphans, all outsiders,' says Coppola, 'but together they formed a family' (quoted in Phillips 2004: 204). This perhaps was the most significant draw of the film for Coppola, given that family is, as Phillips notes, a 'common theme' in Coppola's movies (ibid.). Capturing the sense of loyalty, innocence, and love in the story while keeping out the contempt of Hollywood was key to this project. Coppola found that in order for that to happen, he would need two key things: the right script and the right cast.

Having the right script was turning out to be a harder prospect than Coppola anticipated. He had already selected Rowell to write it, but that process was not unfolding well. Rowell's vision of the film was moving farther and farther from its source material, and Coppola was 'dissatisfied with her adaptation, which, in his view, lost some of the book's charm' (Schumacher 1999: 318). Misakian, who was shown early drafts of the script, agreed with this assessment. Throughout the scriptwriting process, Roos kept her and the students of Lone Star apprised of the progress on the film (see Figure 2.2). 'Fred actually sent us the first script,' Misakian recalled, and she and a teacher shared it with the students – none of whom approved of it in its first iteration. She took it back to him and said, 'We don't like it' (2021).[2] Coppola knew that the kids who signed Misakian's letter wanted to see Hinton's book and characters on screen, not some mutation or Hollywood revision of the novel. He thus fired Rowell and 'decided to do a wholesale rewrite of her screenplay, sticking as closely as possible to the literary source' (Phillips 2004: 204).[3]

It was, after all, the authenticity of Hinton's writing and characters that had drawn him to the project in the first place. In an interview with the *New York Times*, he reflected: 'For me the primary thing about her books is that the characters come across as very real. Her dialogue is memorable, and her prose is striking. Often a paragraph of her descriptive prose sums up something essential and stays with you' (quoted in Farber 1983). Because he regarded Hinton as 'a serious writer' (ibid.), he invited her into the filmmaking process. With her help, he rewrote the script wholesale, straying very little from the original source material. For her part, Hinton recognized how remarkable it was that she was included to the extent that she was: 'I know that I had extremely rare experiences for a writer. Usually the director does not say, "Boys, these are important lines, so you've got to know them word for word," which is what Francis said to the actors. I've been pleased and amazed at my involvement' (quoted in Farber 1983). Hinton's role in helping to bring the film to life is borne out in the opening credits, where she is listed as a "Special Consultant to Francis Coppola."

It is at this point in the process – the writing and casting of the film – that *The Outsiders* begins to take on the characteristics that make it the classic it is today: an adaptation faithful to the original, infused with an authentic narrative voice and adolescent emotion, and a production rooted in Coppola's keen eye for young talent and cultivation of

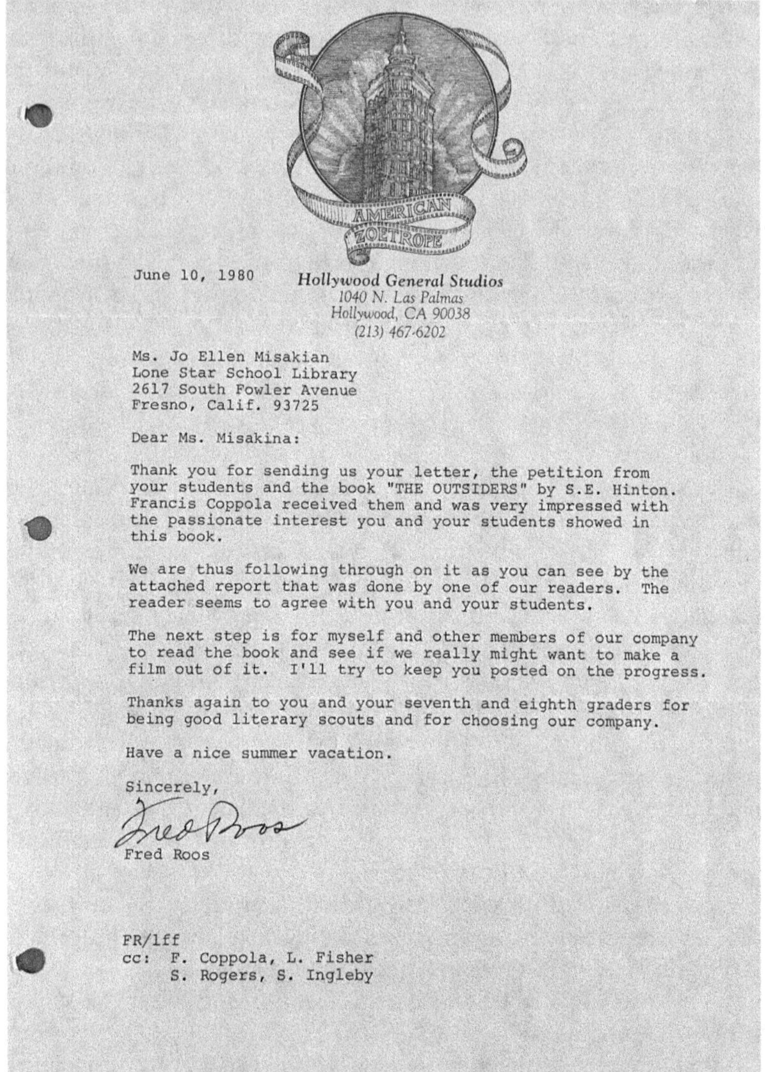

June 10, 1980

Hollywood General Studios
1040 N. Las Palmas
Hollywood, CA 90038
(213) 467-6202

Ms. Jo Ellen Misakian
Lone Star School Library
2617 South Fowler Avenue
Fresno, Calif. 93725

Dear Ms. Misakina:

Thank you for sending us your letter, the petition from your students and the book "THE OUTSIDERS" by S.E. Hinton. Francis Coppola received them and was very impressed with the passionate interest you and your students showed in this book.

We are thus following through on it as you can see by the attached report that was done by one of our readers. The reader seems to agree with you and your students.

The next step is for myself and other members of our company to read the book and see if we really might want to make a film out of it. I'll try to keep you posted on the progress.

Thanks again to you and your seventh and eighth graders for being good literary scouts and for choosing our company.

Have a nice summer vacation.

Sincerely,

Fred Roos

FR/lff
cc: F. Coppola, L. Fisher
S. Rogers, S. Ingleby

Figure 2.2 Producer Fred Roos tells Misakian that the studio will 'keep you posted on the progress,' a promise on which they delivered (Image courtesy of Jo Ellen Misakian)

community. On 1 March 1982, after 14 drafts, Coppola and Hinton had a screenplay ready to go (Phillips 2004: 205; Chown 1988: 163). But before the shooting began, the film had to be cast. And the casting was a story in itself, one that laid the groundwork for the kind of family feeling that would come to define the set of *The Outsiders*.

The Making of *The Outsiders*

In *Hollywood Auteur: Francis Coppola*, Jeffrey Chown observes that '[t]he one aspect of production of *The Outsiders* that seems most typical of the real strength of Coppola as a director is his work with the teenage actors' (1988: 166). To be sure, well before *The Outsiders*, Coppola had established a reputation as a director who enjoyed young people – so much so that his own children were frequently on set and part of his films in various capacities. His oldest child, son Gian-Carlo, played bit roles in Coppola's 1970s films and later worked as an associate producer for both *The Outsiders* and *Rumble Fish* ('Gian-Carlo Coppola: Filmography' no date). His second child, son Roman, also had bit parts in *The Godfather* films and *Apocalypse Now (Redux)*, and he worked as a production assistant on *The Outsiders* ('Roman Coppola: Filmography' no date). His daughter and youngest child, Sofia (now an esteemed director in her own right), began her acting career as the infant Corleone being baptized at the end of *The Godfather* and continued in small roles in *The Outsiders, Rumble Fish*, and *Peggy Sue Got Married* ('Sofia Coppola: Filmography' no date). As an adolescent, she also performed with her dance troupe, the Dingbats, at the Radio City premiere of *One from the Heart* (Ross 2004: 81). The presence and inclusion of Coppola's family in the filmmaking process, in particular his children, was customary from the start of his career; there was little doubt, then, in his ability to select, direct, and collaborate with the young cast of *The Outsiders*.

The selection process, now a famous part of the backstory on *The Outsiders*, was pure Coppola. As he explained in a recent interview in *The Guardian*, 'If my company was famous for anything, it was casting new, unknown actors. I believed in the concept of open casting calls – but I tried to do them in a way that was appropriate for the film we were making' (Hoad 2021). In this case, what he deemed appropriate was gathering 30-plus young male actors in a room together and have them read not just for one specific part but for various roles. The best-known and most entertaining account of the casting of *The Outsiders* appears in Rob Lowe's memoir, *Stories I Only Tell My Friends* (2011). Lowe's recounting of his experiences captures the combination of excitement, confusion, and anxiety that the open casting call produced in him and his friends (and competitors), Emilio Estevez and Tom Cruise. 'A reading for a director is supposed to be a low-key, private meeting,' remembers Lowe. 'This looks like a public cattle call with every important young working actor in the universe' (100). Lowe then describes the audition itself: gathering in a soundstage with chairs against the wall, but not enough chairs for all the actors in the room; opera music blaring as they assemble themselves and prepare to read their lines; the only props in the room consisting of a table and four chairs, with a single light above them. Coppola tells the young actors that '[s]ome of you may be asked to play different roles than you have prepared and some of you won't. This is really just an opportunity to explore the material.' Lowe, still green in the acting world when auditioning for *The Outsiders*, remembers his internal response to Coppola's directions: 'Is he serious?' (103).

Coppola was very serious about this process, a process that allowed him to find just the right actors for these special roles; indeed, as many critics have noted, '[t]he cast of virtual unknowns that Coppola gathered for *The Outsiders* now reads like a Who's Who of the Brat Pack, the hottest young stars of the 1980s' (Bergan 1997: 65). His casting choices for Dallas and Cherry were set from the start: Matt Dillon and Diane Lane were both known quantities at the time and were front-runners for their respective roles. Dillon 'was a shoo-in for alpha greaser Dallas' (Godfrey 2021: 99), oozing his New York style of cool at every audition. Of Lane, Coppola said she 'pretty much had the role from day one because of her beautiful work in *A Little Romance*. I knew she was the right one before we even met her' (quoted in Rice 2021). The other parts, however, were fair game for every actor who auditioned. Janet Hirshenson, a casting director who worked with Coppola on the project, remembers that 'Francis made it clear that he not only wanted Unknowns, he wanted *great* Unknowns – a bunch of fabulous, heart-throb kids with movie star good looks and an authentic kind of toughness that could evoke the alienation and longing so beautifully captured in the novel' (quoted in Hirshenson and Jenkins 2006: 66, italics in original).[4]

In the end, he got them. With the exception of Leif Garrett, who had been a teen idol in the late 1970s, the actors who eventually landed those roles were relative newcomers. C. Thomas Howell and Ralph Macchio had some industry experience to build on: Howell had played a small part in *E.T.* (Spielberg, 1982), while Macchio had played a recurring role on the television series *Eight Is Enough* (ABC, 1977-81).

Like Macchio, Lowe had experience in television with his two appearances in the ABC *Afterschool Specials* (1980-81) but had not yet made his break into movies. Patrick Swayze was best known for his roller-skating prowess in the 1979 film *Skatetown U.S.A.* (Levey), which was enough to get him noticed by Fred Roos and land him the role of Darrel, the oldest character (and actor) on set. Tom Cruise had not yet hit it big with *Risky Business* – that break came months after the release of *The Outsiders* – and before *The Outsiders* had been cast only in smaller roles in *Taps* (Becker, 1981) and *Losin' It* (Hanson, 1982). Darren Dalton and Michelle Meyrink had no acting credits prior to *The Outsiders*. And yet, as Coppola biographer Michael Schumacher notes, '[t]he casting decisions, once again, illustrated Coppola's uncanny knack for placing unknowns in precisely the right roles' (1999: 318). His knack might be better identified as instinct: as a recent article in *Empire* magazine reports of Coppola's process, 'Those who won roles, he says, were the ones he couldn't stop thinking about' (Godfrey 2021: 99).[5]

By the time shooting began in March 1982, a family feeling had already been established by the casting process. This feeling was reinforced by Coppola's production choices, which further recognized the needs of his adolescent cast. Notably, Coppola shot the film according to a chronological schedule. Randy Shanofsky, a veteran cameraman who had his first informal industry experience on the set of *The Outsiders*, explained that this choice was purposeful; filming chronologically would make the experience easier for the young cast. He calls it an 'unbelievable accommodation' (2021), one that underscores Coppola's understanding of how to work effectively with young people.[6] Coppola also understood the importance of getting his cast as much into character as possible, and the way he achieved this is now apocryphal. The young actors were housed in the now-defunct Excelsior Hotel in downtown Tulsa, with those playing the Socs living on the higher floors and the actors playing the Greasers on the lower floors. According to Coppola, the Socs 'got more per diems and stayed in better hotel rooms and were driven in nice cars,' and the Greasers 'had less per diems and lived in less attractive hotel rooms and had crummier cars' (quoted in Godfrey 2021: 100). The Socs were also given personalized bound scripts and leather jackets, whereas the Greasers were given their scripts in three-ring binders (Gilliam et al. 2016). C. Thomas Howell recalls how these strategies stoked rivalry between the actors, allowing them to fully enter their roles: 'There was an envy that was intentionally dialled in to the Soc and Greaser actors' (quoted in Hoad 2021).

The envy did not result in ongoing conflict, however. Rather, what Coppola centered more than anything was the very sense of camaraderie and belonging that the characters in the film were seeking, feelings that he himself had experienced as a young man. 'What I most wanted as a kid was to be part of the group,' says Coppola (quoted in Godfrey 2021: 99). He wanted the same for the kids he had cast in his film. 'Making *The Outsiders*, he says, was a chance to build a group' (ibid.). And what made that group gel – and translated into screen magic that transcends the decades – was his love of and commitment to the story, the storytelling process, and the young cast's development as actors. Many of the bonds that were forged during the filming endure today; Hinton notes how she was close to most of the boys and remains friends with Dillon and Howell in particular. As Howell recalls about the set of *The Outsiders* in an interview, 'It was all fraternal. Everybody was super close and spent a lot of time together, and I think that carried over [into the film]. We all were cut from the same cloth, and I think there's this, I don't know, pride that goes with it' (quoted in Gilliam et al. 2016).

Of course, these bonds were strengthened through Coppola's strategy for encouraging the actors to fully enter into their roles as Greasers and Socs. The aforementioned production choices were one way that he reinforced the class differences essential to the characterization and plot of *The Outsiders*. He also pushed the actors to inhabit their roles by living them, even if briefly; he believed that a director's job is to 'give them experiences that help them unlock the characters' (Godfrey 2021: 100). Lowe recalls how he and Tom Cruise were sent to the home of some 'real Greasers' as an immersive learning experiences (2011: 123). Similarly, Ralph Macchio, deemed 'too Long Island' and 'too happy family' for Coppola, was given five dollars and told to spend the night outside. Macchio recalls how Coppola 'gave me stuff to think about and it really helped – walking in the shoes of a kid who's got no place to go, and nowhere to sleep, and his parents aren't there to back him up, and he's got a few dollars in his pocket, and that's it' (quoted in Gilliam et al. 2016). To inhabit the role of Dally, Coppola suggested that Matt Dillon spend the night in jail; the young actor refused, saying, 'Ok, Francis, why don't *you* go spend the night in jail?' (quoted in 'Staying Gold' 2005). Yet Dillon contributed to the family feeling of the young cast in his own way: by pulling numerous pranks at the hotel. As Susan King notes in 'The Outsiders Stays Gold at 35,' 'The tales of the pranks and shenanigans that went on at the Excelsior Hotel [...] are stuff of legend' (2018). Howell came home one night to find everything in his room turned upside down; Diane Lane had her bed short-sheeted and various surfaces of her hotel room covered in honey and Vaseline (King 2018); Lowe and Cruise engaged in sparring sessions in the hotel hallway, and many of the boys participated in the 'nightly flyby of the lobby to check out any potential girl activity' (Lowe 2011: 134, 135). In other words, the young actors were not prevented from indulging in youthful immaturity at the right moment; paradoxically, that immaturity was essential to the characters they were to inhabit on the set.

While the boys were enjoying their adolescence, Coppola was at the helm, functioning as the patriarch of the wily unit of young actors. As the director and paterfamilias, Coppola struck a figure at once imposing and inviting. On the one hand, here was the man who had created *The Godfather* and *Apocalypse Now*, two of the greatest cinematic epics of the 1970s, working with a group of young actors all hoping to make it big in Hollywood. Being cast in *The Outsiders* – and even more so, being directed by Coppola – was a dream come true for many of them. In his memoir, Lowe recalls how Coppola could be 'aloof' and 'play favorites' (2011: 137), yet in the moment, young Lowe wanted nothing more than to earn his approval: 'Like everyone else, I do whatever I can to please him, make him proud, and to be in his good graces' (ibid.). While Coppola allowed the young actors to engage in hijinks off set, on set he maintained high standards for his actors; Lowe recalls the 'lengthy, sometimes bizarre' rehearsal processes that led to 14-hour days during shooting (128). The director's hand may have been demanding, but not heavy. Indeed, Lowe describes how that in the midst of filming, 'Francis is really grinding us, but we love it' (130), ultimately noting how 'my most influential teacher was Coppola' (128). C. Thomas Howell likewise recalls how 'Coppola was a real patriarch for everybody, the entire cast and crew. He'd make meals for us at lunchtime and spend a lot of time telling us stories about other films that he made [...] it was a good time for us to have a mentor like Coppola' (quoted in Gilliam et al. 2016). It makes sense that Dillon referred to Coppola as 'Father Film' during the shooting of *The Outsiders* (Schumacher 1999: 323). Coppola was a father of film and a father of *this* film – and thus in a sense, their father during the filming.

If Coppola was the dad on the set of *The Outsiders*, then Hinton was the mom. She was, after all, the woman who had birthed the story to begin with. As noted earlier, because Coppola so valued Hinton's work as a writer, he invited her to participate in the film's production – a move that at the time was 'very unusual' in Hollywood (Shanofsky

Figure 2.3 Hinton and Coppola, mom and dad on the set, scout locations together (Image courtesy of S.E. Hinton)

2021). Hinton also remembers how early in the process, Coppola 'came to town to scout locations. I scouted locations with him' (quoted in Korfhage 2017). One of the most charming pictures from the filming of *The Outsiders* – a photo on display in The Outsiders House Museum in Tulsa – is a candid shot of Coppola and Hinton on a bike, cheerfully riding through the neighborhood where the movie would eventually be filmed (see Figure 2.3). 'I loved working with Francis,' Hinton told a reporter years later (quoted in Korfhage 2017). The most important role she played, however, was her self-described role as 'greaser den mother.' Recognizing that most of the boys were in fact still boys, not mature men who could care for themselves, and that '[n]one of them had any parental supervision,' Hinton says she 'took it upon myself to look after them' (quoted in Godfrey 2021: 100). Darren Dalton, who played Soc Randy in the film, recalls how Hinton 'was very motherly to all of us on the set in the best way' (quoted in Gilliam et al. 2016). As Hinton herself mused, 'I really bonded with my greaser boys' (quoted in Korfhage 2017).

With father Coppola and mother Hinton at the helm, the feeling on the set of *The Outsiders* was that of a family unit. Per Coppola, the production 'was headquartered in a high school; we had all of our stuff with us, it was akin to, "Let's put on a show"' (quoted in Ramsey 2005: E14). Macchio recalls that 'Coppola had a very theatrical way of working. We spent two weeks really improvising things, doing different scenes, doing acting exercises. He was very much about the camaraderie, so when we shot the movie, we felt like we had been with each other a little bit' (quoted in Gilliam et al. 2016). And in the end, they did put on a show: whether that show involved morning tai chi, acrobat and tumbling lessons in a local gym, or fighting each other for fun in the hotel, the cast and crew got along beautifully. Hinton recalls, 'There wasn't any infighting, there wasn't any backstabbing and nobody was gossiping [...] They were cohesive' (quoted in Graham 2017). As a recent article in *Empire* magazine concludes: 'Everybody loved making *The Outsiders*' (Godfrey 2021: 100). The love that was central to the filming of the movie was also central to the narrative of the film itself, as I will discuss in the next chapter.

From Production to Big Screen

Shooting for *The Outsiders* wrapped on 15 May 1982, and the following months were spent on post-production work in preparation for the film's target release date of October 1982. Such a target date, falling as it would during the holiday movie season, would position the film perfectly for box office success. But Warner Bros.' response to Coppola's work threw a wrench in the plans. As Schumacher explains, the studio 'didn't like Coppola's edited version of *The Outsiders* any more than the rough cut that he had showed them earlier in the year' (1999: 331). Firm in their belief that young people would be bored by a teen movie with a two-hour running time, the studio insisted that Coppola edit the film even more. They wanted 'a polished, highly commercial teen flick that ran no more than an hour and a half' (ibid.), and in the end, Coppola had to cut over 20 minutes of footage from the film (Phillips 2010b: 198), thereby compromising his original depth of characterization. Disappointed in Coppola's work and distrustful of the film's potential for commercial viability, Warner Bros. ultimately postponed the release date to spring of 1983 (Schumacher 1999: 331). Lowe recalls how he was 'too green in the ways of the business to understand that when a big movie moves off a Christmas release date, it's a sign of trouble' (2011: 161).

The trouble was not what Coppola focused on when discussing the film in interviews, however. Rather, he repeatedly stressed the epic nature of the movie, thereby aligning it both with the kinds of films he had already made as a director and with other Hollywood classics. Noting that *The Outsiders* was adapted from a 'a book of big scale, of proportion – a tragedy,' Coppola described the film as a '"Gone With the Wind" for 14-year-old girls' and 'a "Godfather" for children' (quoted in McCarthy 1982: 172). Coppola critic Gene D. Phillips suggests that the filmmaker 'envisioned the movie to be like *Gone with the Wind*, not so much in content as in style' (2004: 206).[7] The style, which Coppola himself described as 'lavish' (quoted in Thomas and Gray 1983: 65), was best conveyed through the director's choice to film *The Outsiders* 'in widescreen and color in order to recreate the world of romantic melodrama' (Phillips 2010a: 195). At the same time, the use of Panavision represented a nod to 'the genre's hallmark work, *Rebel Without a Cause*' (Lewis 1995: 100). In other words, through his choices vis-à-vis *The Outsiders*, Coppola was doing two things at once: creating an epic film and presenting his entry into the burgeoning genre of youth cinema of the early 1980s. As Jeffrey Chown observes of the final product: '[t]he lyrical, but overwrought visuals of *The Outsiders* evoked the exaggerated desperation of the teenage years, unleavened by adult experience' (1988: 154).

'Teenage years, unleavened by adult experience': this phrase could be used to describe many films in the teen cinema genre. Thus, to conclude this chapter, I want to situate *The Outsiders* film within the historical moment of its release: the early 1980s in Hollywood cinema. On 13 August 1982, *Fast Times at Ridgemont High* hit theaters; it became a surprise smash success, earning $27 million dollars at the U.S. box office, six times its actual budget ('*Fast Times at Ridgemont High*: Summary' no date). Likewise, one of the raunchiest entries in the teen film genre, *Porky's*, was released on 19 March 1982; its enormous success at the box office led Paramount to release a sequel, *Porky's II*, on 24 June 1983. *Risky Business* was only months away from its release on 5 August 1983, thereby changing the landscape of teen films and of Tom Cruise's career. Almost a year after *The Outsiders*, *Footloose* (Ross) was released on 17 February 1984. And John Hughes was about to have the first of his many '80s teen hits with *Sixteen Candles*, which hit theaters on 4 May 1984. Weeks after *The Outsiders* was released on 25 March 1983, another very different youth-oriented film, *Flashdance* (Lyne) came to the big screen on 15 April 1983 and took over the number one spot. As Jon Lewis notes of this era, 'the teen audience was a prodigious market at the time – audience studies indicated that four out of every ten teenagers went to the movies at least once a month and that 73% of all ticket sales could be attributed to the twelve-to-twenty-nine-year-old target market' (1995: 104). The teen market was ready, and *The Outsiders* was ready to appeal to that market.

Taken within the context of other youth movies of the era – *Fast Times at Ridgemont High, Porky's, Risky Business*, and the Hughes movies to come – *The Outsiders* was an outlier in many ways. It was an outlier first and foremost in terms of genre: a melodrama in a sea of teenage comedies. It was, too, in terms of its setting: a story of class conflict and belonging set 20 years in the past. By way of comparison within the realm of teen movies, it is worth considering Coppola side by side with John Hughes. No director is more associated with 1980s teen films than Hughes. He captured a very specific historical/cultural moment, best represented in two of his biggest commercial successes: *Sixteen Candles* and *The Breakfast Club*. Coppola's contribution to the teen genre contains virtually nothing of the Hughes aesthetic: teen actors living very much in the present, dealing with embarrassing or overbearing parents, the drama of high school, and raging hormones. In contrast, Coppola captured the affective experience of the coming-of-age process with a film made in the 1980s but lacking most of the specificity that already characterized the genre. Indeed, the only immediately recognizable 1980s characteristic of the film is the actors themselves, 'male stars who would dominate the next generation of movies' (Lowe 2011: 166). As Janet Hirshenson asserts, '[t]he contrast between traditional Hollywood teen fare and *The Outsiders* couldn't have been stronger' (Hirshenson and Jenkins 2006: 86). In so many ways, *The Outsiders* was an outsider in the teen film genre, distinguished by both its form and its feeling. It is to these that I turn my attention in the next chapter.

Notes

1 Over the course of his career, Coppola has changed his name twice. In her 1982 interview, Lillian Ross observes that 'Francis Coppola was originally known as Francis Ford Coppola, having been named after the *Hour* and his father's boss. A few years ago, Mr. Coppola decided that he liked his name better without the Ford. Distributors, however, are still attached to it, and use it in his name most of the time' (2004: 70). Throughout the 1980s, Coppola went by the shortened name. By 1990, when he directed *The Godfather Part III*, he had returned to his full name. Currently, both his winery and his star on the Hollywood Walk of Fame likewise feature his full name.

2 The extent to which Misakian and the students were involved is remarkable. Throughout the process, according to Misakian, 'Fred kept us informed of every move' (2021) – a relationship that cemented the movie's relationship to youth culture. Recognizing the crucial role that Misakian and the Lone Star students played in the creation of the film, Coppola dedicated the movie to them and Warner Bros. flew the stars of *The Outsiders* to the school for a preview of the film (Harmetz).

3 Though Coppola wrote the script, he ultimately was not given credit for doing so. Coppola explained, 'in the Writers Guild rules, they weigh very heavily for the first person to do an adaptation [...] the Guild ruled against me getting any credit, even though I sat down and wrote the script that I used' (quoted in Schumacher 1999: 324).

4 The audition list for *The Outsiders* included an impressive lineup of both established and up-and-coming young male actors: Scott Baio, Nicolas Cage, Robert Downey Jr., Dennis Quaid, and Mickey Rourke (the last of whom would go on to star as the Motorcycle Boy in Coppola's *Rumble Fish*) (Lowe 2011: 104 and Hoad 2021).

5 There was a practical side to Coppola's casting choices as well: it was cheaper. As Phillips notes, Coppola 'cast promising young actors in the picture who did not yet command big salaries' (2004: 204).

6 For the delightful story of how Shanofsky was invited to the set by S.E. Hinton's husband David Inhofe, see Bob Carlson's (2018) podcast 'Unfictional: The Outsider.'

7 Coppola often commented on how, in content and style, his two Hinton adaptations paralleled his two epic films. *The Outsiders* 'was a romantic melodrama along the lines of *The Godfather*, while he envisioned *Rumble Fish* as an art film, designed more in the direction of *Apocalypse Now*' (Phillips 2004: 225).

3 Form and Feeling in *The Outsiders*

When thinking about teen films of the early 1980s, a collection of very specific and now-iconic images and narratives often comes to mind: Linda Barrett in her red bikini, emerging wet from a backyard pool and removing her top in seductive slow motion. Joel Goodson with his toothy grin and Ray-Bans, scheming at once to lose his virginity and to get into Princeton. Sam Baker rolling her eyes in outrage over her family's forgetfulness of her birthday and biting her lip in unrequited love of football star Jake Ryan. A group of white, gangly teenage boys with names like Pee Wee and Meat, peering through the hole in a locker room shower in the hopes of getting a glimpse of naked young women. What all of these films have in common is one of two things: sex or romance (or both), the essential ingredients of the typical '80s teen film. Timothy Shary notes that '[m]ost Hollywood films about youth in the 1980s relied on formulas that exploited youth issues, specifically sexual development' (2014: 22). Most youth films – but not *The Outsiders*. Rather, Coppola's movie was a throwback to an earlier time – the era of *Rebel Without a Cause* – and thus was comprised of a remarkably different content: not teen sex and not romance, but young men's attempts to find themselves with the help of a surrogate family. Given its content, where does *The Outsiders* fit in the canon of 1980s teen movies?

While teen films have a long history in Hollywood – cataloged in different ways by landmark studies such as David M. Considine's *The Cinema of Adolescence* (1985), Jon Lewis's *The Road to Romance and Ruin* (1992), Thomas Doherty's *Teenagers and Teenpics* (2002), Catherine Driscoll's *Teen Film: A Critical Introduction* (2011), and Timothy Shary's *Generation Multiplex* (2014) – most scholars agree that it was in the 1980s that the teen film found its grounding as a genre. Shary asserts that 'the 1980s were perhaps the most fertile period of teen films in American history' (2005: 3). Frances Smith, in *Rethinking the Hollywood Teen Movie*, concurs, stating that 'the 1980s was the decade

DOI: 10.4324/9781003228783-4

in which the teen movie calcified into a coherent genre' (2017: 14). Many scholars attribute the boom in teen films in the 1980s to the ways in which 'teenagers had become sophisticated, savvy consumers, highly attuned to the commoditised, market-driven society in which they were growing up' (Christie 2009: 63). As a response to this burgeoning consumer base, the teen film flourished, 'profiting from exploring broader themes relevant to a youth audience, such as sex, drugs, class conflict, and gender politics" (Lewis 2016: 7).

One thematic element of *The Outsiders* that places it squarely in the canon of 1980s teen films is its focus on the 'stark social divide of teen society' (Lewis 2016: 7). Indeed, journalist Hadley Freeman describes how many teen films of the era 'were completely overt in their treatment of [class]: class is the major motivator of plot [...] They stress that true class mobility is pretty much impossible, and certainly interclass friendships and romances are unlikely, for the simple reason that rich people are assholes and lower-middle-class and working-class people are good' (Freeman 2015: 184). Freeman's assessment is as accurate as it is sarcastic. With its depiction of the poverty experienced by the Greasers and the privileges enjoyed by the Socs, *The Outsiders* 'deal[s] realistically with kids from the wrong side of the tracks' (Hirshenson and Jenkins 2006: 88).[1] As such, it can be grouped with other teen films of the era that represent the conflict borne of the socioeconomic differences between peer groups: several films from John Hughes's oeuvre, including *The Breakfast Club* (1985), *Pretty in Pink* (Deutch, 1986), and *Some Kind of Wonderful* (Deutch, 1987); *Can't Buy Me Love* (Rash, 1987); *Dirty Dancing* (Ardolino, 1987); and *Say Anything...* (Crowe, 1989).

The film's treatment of social class is perhaps one of the *only* ways in which *The Outsiders* parallels other teen films of the era, however. In addition to the above observations by Lewis and Freeman, most scholars of the genre also agree that '[t]he contradiction between maturity and immaturity that "teen" thus describes is central to teen film' (Driscoll 2011: 2). The immaturity is often displayed through the protagonists' relationship to gender, race, sexual orientation, romance, and especially sexual activity. Shary observes that in the wake of the success of *Porky's*, many early '80s movies focused thematically on sex – from a male point of view. 'By the 1980s,' Shary notes, 'the new sexist mythology of movies told boys they no longer had to join gangs or drive fast cars to act like men, they just had to treat girls as sexual conquests' (2014: 48). Smith, citing Jane Feuer, likewise observes how the 'genre consists principally in a "sexual coming of age narrative"' (2017: 3) – and this coming-of-age process most often focused on boys' sexuality.

It is on this landscape that Coppola's film makes its debut. When *The Outsiders* was released in March 1983, the genre of the teen film had already been identified as an emerging powerhouse in the movie industry. Scholars now recognize how, primarily as a result of its cast and its renowned director, *The Outsiders* solidified and legitimized the genre, paving the way for future teen movies of the 1980s.[2] Thomas A. Christie notes how *The Outsiders*, alongside early-80s films such as *Times Square* (Moyle, 1980) and *Flashdance*, was among a handful of early 1980s teen films that 'showcased uniquely different aspects of the teen consciousness of the new decade, and rang the changes around the now-dated genre films which had originated from the seventies' (2009: 63) – films such as *American Graffiti* (Lucas, 1973) and *Grease* (Kleiser, 1978). Shary likewise asserts that 'the greatest influence of *The Outsiders* [is] in its elevation of teen experience to serious standards' (2022). It is the film's seriousness, or what I identified at the end of Chapter 2 as its combination of form and feeling, that distinguishes it from most other teen films of the era. In terms of form, Coppola clearly reaches back to and echoes a handful of classic films, most notably *Rebel Without a Cause*. In terms of feeling, *The Outsiders* privileges a theme and representation that is rare in '80s teen films: intimacy between young men, independent of sexual escapades. This is due in part to Coppola's faithfulness to Hinton's book, reflecting the closeness and emotional bonds between the young boys. But it is also due in part to Coppola's filmmaking techniques. With his choice of Panavision, his privileging of close-ups, and his narrative foregrounding of emotion and sentiment rather than sex, Coppola's movie hearkens back to a genre that is typically associated with femininity: the melodrama. In the remainder of this chapter, I discuss form and feeling in *The Outsiders*, underscoring the uniqueness of Coppola's movie both as a teen film and within the genre in the 1980s, and concluding with a brief discussion of how its unusual combination of gender and genre impacted the reception of the film.

Form: Looking Back to Old Hollywood

Most teen films of the early '80s are set firmly in their historical moment: they feature the most popular fashion, cars, and music of the era. Movies like *Fast Times at Ridgemont High* and *Valley Girl* (Coolidge, 1983) also represent a specific geographical area (in this case, Southern California), and the clothes and dialogue and soundtracks underscore this. And most take place in a high school, the location seen as the center of teen life in the 1980s. Indeed, high school films are 'the most foundational subgenre of youth films'

(Shary 2014: 11). *The Outsiders* does not check any of these teen film boxes. Released in 1983, it takes place in the mid-1960s in Tulsa, Oklahoma, a geographical location without the charisma and contemporary cachet of SoCal. The fashion and cars are a throwback – t-shirts, rolled jeans, mustangs, and madras – and the music, discussed more below, evinces no trace of 1980s pop or new wave sound. The characters' high school is peripheral, mentioned in passing and featured in a single scene only in the 2005 *Complete Novel* version of the film. As I will discuss in Chapter 4, the film's connection to and reflection of the 1980s lies almost solely in its cast, which featured almost all of the up-and-coming male actors of the era, many of whom would soon be known as the 'Brat Pack.'

Aesthetically, *The Outsiders* reflects not the 1980s but films of the 1950s and 1960s, reaching back to Hollywood classics for its inspiration. Its aesthetic begins with its score. One of the hallmarks of 1980s teen films is their soundtrack. Jackson Browne's 'Somebody's Baby' became the unofficial theme of *Fast Times at Ridgemont High*; Bob Seger's 'Old Time Rock and Roll' defined the now-iconic scene from *Risky Business*. *Fame* (Parker, 1980) and *Flashdance* had theme songs by Irene Cara; Modern English's 'I Melt With You' became synonymous with *Valley Girl*; and *Sixteen Candles* was bookended by two indie hits, Altered Images' 'Happy Birthday' and The Thompson Twins' 'If You Were Here.' James King, Timothy Shary, and Frances Smith all discuss how the 1980s became the decade in which movies and music developed the most synergistic of relationships, thanks to the debut of MTV in 1981. King explains how films in the early 1980s 'began to be influenced by the growing popularity of music videos' (2018: 73). Examining MTV's influence across the decade, Smith, referencing the research of Kay Dickinson, notes how MTV 'shaped the aesthetic style of the teen film itself' (2017: 15). To be sure, it is challenging to think of an '80s teen film without humming tunes from its corresponding '80s soundtrack.

Unless, of course, that film is *The Outsiders*. No '80s tunes populate this soundtrack – except the original song that plays over the opening credits, 'Stay Gold,' sung by Stevie Wonder and composed by Wonder and Carmine Coppola, Francis's father. But 'Stay Gold' sounds nothing like a pop song from 1983. It features no synthesizer, no drum machines, no stylish accompanying music video; only the heartfelt voice of Wonder singing about innocence and fleeting youth: 'Life is but a twinkling of an eye/Yet filled with sorrow and compassion/Though not imagined, all things that happen/Will age too old/Though gold.' And 'Stay Gold' bears the hallmark of the rest of the score of *The Outsiders*: the sincere, sweeping sound of Carmine Coppola's score. In interviews, Francis Coppola repeatedly refers to his father's score as 'schmaltzy,' a term that suggests a purposeful throwback to older cinema:

> The key to *The Outsiders* is the score; the fact that it's this schmaltzy classical movie score indicates that I wanted a movie told in sumptuous terms, very honestly or carefully taken from the book without changing it a lot, with young actors – putting the emphasis more on that kind of *Gone with the Wind* lyricism which was so important to the young girl [Susie Hinton] when she wrote it.
>
> (quoted in Thomson and Gray 1983: 62, brackets in original)

At least one review of the film, in *Variety*, recognized this throwback but aligned the musical aesthetic not with *Gone with the Wind* but two other classic films: the 'highly dramatic score [...] evokes Leonard Rosenman's work on the James Dean pics "Rebel Without a Cause" and "East of Eden"' ('Review of *The Outsiders*' 1983: 18). Similarly, Coppola scholar Jeffrey Chown observes how the 'over-emotional, exaggerated, melodramatic sound' echoes older films, though he identifies it as an 'imitation *West Side Story* score' (1988: 164). In calling his father's work a 'soaring, romantic score' (quoted in Hoad 2021), Coppola gave his viewers a sense of the feeling he was trying to capture: one of classic films, big movies with big stories, and big images to match.

Even in the 2005 re-release of the film, *The Complete Novel*, in which Coppola replaces his father's score with more era-appropriate music because he concluded that his father's work was 'too dense,' Coppola deviates from the early 1980s teen film formula. There is no Jackson Browne or Irene Cara in this newly-edited film, but instead, in the words of Coppola, 'more of what the Greasers would have listened to' (quoted in Hoad 2021): Elvis Presley, Carl Perkins, and Jerry Lee Lewis among others. In his study of nostalgia in '80s movies, Michael D. Dwyer observes how '[f]ilm and popular music are both significant sites for the production of nostalgia [...] music can act as a powerful generator of memory and marker of generational belonging' (2015: 13). Even with its throwback score, however, *The Outsiders* resists categorization as a nostalgia film in the vein of earlier teen films such as *American Graffiti* and *Grease* or later ones such as *Stand By Me* (Reiner, 1986) or *Dirty Dancing*. The songs in *The Outsiders* function less as 'marker[s] of generational belonging' than as evocative markers of the setting. And when identifying the movie's setting, both those who saw the original version, such as *New York Times* critic Michiko Kakutani (1984: 1) and those who studied the film after the release of the *Complete Novel*, are mistaken about when the film takes place. Dwyer, for example, joins Kakutani in claiming that *The Outsiders* takes place in the 1950s (2015: 80). Based on this, I would argue that the film is characterized by an ambiguity vis-à-vis its era, an ambiguity that tempers its invitation to indulge in nostalgia. Coppola specifically notes how the music in the *Complete Novel* edition of the film is meant to represent the songs the characters would listen to – not songs that would take the audience back to their youth. The only song on the soundtrack that would accurately transport audiences to the historical moment in which the teen characters are living is Van Morrison's 1964 hit 'Gloria,' released a year before the movie is set.

With or without what Coppola describes as 'early Elvis Presley and stuff like that' (in Hoad 2021), virtually all aspects of *The Outsiders* as a film – from its score and cinematography to its casting and composition – echo earlier movies. There are obvious references to *Gone With the Wind*, which I discuss later in the chapter, but narratively and visually *The Outsiders* as teen movie is most aligned with Nicholas Ray's 1955 film *Rebel Without a Cause*. Shary notes that '[t]he influence of *Rebel Without a Cause* [on teen films] is difficult to underestimate' (2005: 21), and that influence extended well into the 1980s.[3] The most discernable connection is the plot, which is straight out of a juvenile delinquent (JD) film: with its focus on 'youth crime,' 'anti-social behaviour,' and the 'framing of such behaviour as a *social problem* – a problem that requires both explanations and remedial actions to prevent it' (Buckingham no date, italics in original), *The Outsiders* often 'feels very much like a 1950s drama about problem kids, such as those directed by Nicolas Ray and Elia Kazan' ('Review of *The Outsiders*' 1983: 18). But plot alone does not establish the cinematic connection to *Rebel Without a Cause*. Coppola scholar Jon Lewis asserts that the director's 'evocative use of wide-screen Panavision' was 'an obvious allusion to the genre's hallmark work, *Rebel Without a Cause*' (1995: 100). To be sure, Coppola conceived 'the film adaptation as a Technicolor widescreen melodrama' (Burns 2018). A cousin of the CinemaScope of *Rebel Without a Cause*, Panavision at once contributed to the lush visual appearance of *The Outsiders* and mirrored its cinematic predecessor. From its wide-screen images to its vibrant color to its close-ups of the young actors, *The Outsiders* features many scenes that mimic the look of *Rebel Without a Cause,* scenes that highlight intense feelings (see Figures 3.1 and 3.2). Cinematographer Steven Burum acknowledges how in shooting the film, he and Coppola were 'trying to do a stylistic thing that's evocative of movies of that time' (quoted in 'Staying Gold' 2005). In both *Rebel Without a Cause* and *The Outsiders*, the cinematography and style create an aesthetic that privileges emotion, a point to which I will return later in the chapter.

Equally significant is the casting. Both in character and in appearance, Matt Dillon as Dallas Winston and Ralph Macchio as Johnny Cade explicitly hearken back to the iconic actors and their roles in *Rebel Without a Cause*: James Dean as Jim Stark and Sal Mineo as Plato Crawford, respectively. In its review of *The Outsiders, Variety* suggested that the '[w]hole passage of [Johnny and Ponyboy's] isolation reminds forcibly of the Sal Mineo-James Dean relationship in "Rebel Without a Cause"' ('Review of *The Outsiders*' 1983: 18). Based on casting and

Figure 3.1 Jim Stark's cry for help to his parents: 'You're tearing me apart!'

Figure 3.2 Dally's cry for help to Johnny: 'C'mon, Johnny, don't die on me now!'

characterization, however, it is more accurate to align Johnny and Dally with the Plato-Jim relationship. As I will discuss in greater depth in Chapter 4, Dillon was marketed as a James Dean-type actor, a sensitive bad boy. In an interview, Roger Ebert told Dillon that in *The Outsiders*, he 'played for this generation the kinds of characters that Brando, James Dean and Elvis Presley once represented for their generations' (1983a). An article in *Tulsa World* likewise identified Dillon as the actor who 'portrayed the troubled young rebels of Hinton's novels with the passion and anger of a young James Dean' (King 2019). Side-by-side shots of the two films likewise illustrate the parallels between Dean and Dillon (see Figures 3.3 and 3.4): cool, sensitive loners with a cigarette in hand. Coppola further underscored these parallels with the casting of Ralph Macchio as Johnny. In a review of *The Outsiders*, film critic Lawrence

Figures 3.3 and 3.4 Whether lighting up before the chickee run or an outing to the drive-in, Jim and Dally exude cool

Figures 3.5 and 3.6 Plato and Johnny, 'doe-eyed and tremulous': the most vulnerable characters in *Rebel Without a Cause* and *The Outsiders*

O'Toole called Macchio a 'Sal Mineo prototype – doe-eyed and tremulous' (1983: 62). To be sure, Macchio's portrayal of Johnny, combined with his resemblance to Sal Mineo, cements the overlay between *Rebel Without a Cause* and *The Outsiders* (see Figures 3.5 and 3.6). The characters share both a touching vulnerability and an admiration of the alpha 'rebel' males in their worlds, Jim and Dally.

Writing about *The Outsiders*, Jean-Paul Chaillet and Elizabeth Vincent observe that 'Coppola is perhaps the only film director who can create an original work while still paying tribute to past masters, and never stray into areas of plagiarism' (1984: 98). Through its combination of score, casting, and cinematography, *The Outsiders* recognized the influence of and, in many ways, paid tribute to *Rebel Without a Cause.*

In doing so, it established itself as a teen movie with a richer cinematic lineage than most films of the era, as well as more heft than its contemporaries. With Coppola in the director's chair, *The Outsiders* was arguably the most elevated Hollywood youth movie of the 1980s.

Feeling: *The Outsiders* as Melodrama

Just as significant as the visual similarity between the two films is their shared generic heritage: the melodrama.[4] In his essay 'Melodrama and Tears,' Steve Neale discusses how the genre is primarily characterized 'by emotional hyperbole, by what Peter Brooks has called "grandiose emotional states"' (1986: 12). Given both films' emphasis on intense feeling, their categorization as melodramas makes sense. Beyond this simple definition, however, they differ from each other in terms of the *type* of melodrama they are. *Rebel Without a Cause* is widely considered a family melodrama: a genre that focuses on the middle-class family and 'exposes the tensions and contradictions that lie beneath the surface of post-war suburban American life' (Mercer and Shingler 2004: 2). In his book *Hollywood Genres: Formulas, Filmmaking, and the Studio System*, Thomas Schatz further classifies *Rebel Without a Cause* as a male melodrama or a 'male weepie,' a subcategory of the 1950s family melodrama in which 'the central conflict involves passing the role of middle-class American "Dad" from one generation to the next' (1981: 239). Schatz identifies James Dean as the 'master of the tormented-son portrayal' in this sub-genre (ibid.). Though a family melodrama *par excellence*, *Rebel Without a Cause*'s emotionally wrought narrative centers in large part on masculinity, on Jim Stark's desperate desire to find a model of acceptable manhood in his father.

The primary concern of the male melodrama – 'the need for the male protagonist to assume, in some for or other, the role of patriarch within a family unit' (Mercer and Shingler 2004: 98) – is not at the center of *The Outsiders*. Whether viewers consider Ponyboy, Johnny, or Dally the male protagonist, it is difficult to argue that their main motivation throughout the film is to enter into the role of 'patriarch within a family unit.' For this reason, I contend that *The Outsiders* is not a male melodrama but rather is aligned more explicitly with the melodrama as a female film form. Coppola called *The Outsiders* a 'melodrama with a romantic tone' (quoted in Thompson and Gray 1983: 61), a description that explicitly evokes melodrama's association with the feminine. This association has a long history in cinema. In her brief survey of the development of Hollywood melodrama, Christine Gledhill describes how the advent of talking pictures brought with it clear lines of demarcation between film genres. As

Gledhill explains, 'the power of speech instituted a critical break between a cinema destined for realism and its melodramatic origins' (1987b: 34). With this new privileging of film as a realist medium, 'critical boundary lines' were drawn between genres: 'The "classic" genres were constructed by recourse to masculine cultural values – gangster as "tragic hero"; the "epic" of the West; "adult" realism – while "melodrama" was acknowledged only in those denigrated reaches of the juvenile and the popular' – that is, the 'feminised spheres' (ibid.). In her book *American Film Cycles*, Amanda Ann Klein observes how since the 1970s, film scholars have reinforced this connotation: 'melodrama has become interchangeable with terms like "soap opera," "tearjerker," and "woman's film" [...], implying that these are films dealing with the domestic, the intimate, and heightened emotions rather than the public, the exterior, and actions' (2011: 38-9). Klein summarizes how, as a result, 'we tend to think of melodrama as being emotionally manipulative, over the top, feminine, and unrealistic' (38). Domestic, intimate, emotional: not adjectives we would immediately associate with tough Greasers. Yet Coppola's own characterization of *The Outsiders* invites audiences to do so.

It is not Coppola's description alone that classifies *The Outsiders* as a melodrama, however. Characterization, setting, and plot reflect the conventions of the genre as well. In terms of characterization, according to Martha Vicinus, '[m]elodrama always sides with the powerless' (quoted in Gledhill 1987b: 14). The first-person narrative framework of *The Outsiders* – bookended as it is by the image of Ponyboy at his desk, writing the essay for his English teacher – situates Ponyboy as the central protagonist with whom audiences are meant to identify, or at least trust. And Ponyboy, the youngest of the Greasers, is most certainly vulnerable by virtue of his age, his social class, and his identity as an orphan. The other Greasers, too, are powerless, but none more so than Johnny. According to Thomas Elsaesser, '[o]ne of the characteristic features of melodramas in general is that they concentrate on the point of view of the victim' (1987: 64), and though Ponyboy is the narrator and most certainly a victim, *The Outsiders* positions Johnny as the most victimized of the group and the Greaser most deserving of our sympathy. When Johnny recognizes Bob as the Soc who mercilessly beat him, Coppola frames his terrified face in a close-up (see Figure 3.6); he does the same after Johnny has killed Bob in self-defense. In those instances audiences, too, are invited to feel his terror.

Elsaesser additionally observes how '[m]elodrama is iconographically fixed by the claustrophobic atmosphere of the bourgeois home and/or the small-town setting' (1987: 62). While the 'bourgeois home' is not the site of action in *The Outsiders*, the blue-collar home most certainly is, a topic that I discuss further in Chapter 5. But the 'small-town setting' of the film, Tulsa in the 1960s, is indeed claustrophobic; the closed world of the Greasers consists of the movie theater, the drive-in, the park, and the Curtis brothers' house. As one review notes, 'there's little sense of time or place' in the film (Sragow 1983: 55); the film is set in 'anyplace and anytime, any medium-sized contemporary town' (Wood 1994: 107). There is nothing that distinguishes their world as unique or dynamic; they are stuck in it just as the female protagonist in classic Hollywood melodramas is stuck in the home. Finally, there is the plot. As a genre, the melodrama often relies on an exaggerated, emotional plot rife with familial, romantic, and/or social conflict, concluding with 'a definitive feeling of loss, which often drives the viewer to tears' (Klein 2011: 41). Summarizing the work of Linda Williams, Klein observes that 'the revelation of truth in a melodrama is often marked through a visual tableau – a moment in which it is either "in the nick of time" or "too late" for a character with whom the audience has been encouraged to identify' (40). We see such a tableau in the final moments of *The Outsiders*, when Ponyboy reads the letter that Johnny has left for him (see Figure 3.7). In it, Johnny asks Ponyboy to tell Dally to look at the sunset and think about 'how there's still lots of good in the world' – and of course, it is too late to do so, as Dally too is now dead.

But it is not just characterization, setting, and plot that distinguish *The Outsiders* as a melodrama. All aspects of form – the choice of Panavision, the cinematography, and importantly, further generic conventions – contribute to and create feeling. In his foundational essay on the genre, 'Tales of Sound and Fury,' Thomas Elsaesser asserts that when '[c]onsidered as an expressive code, melodrama might [...] be described as a particular form of dramatic *mise en scène*,

Figure 3.7 Too late for Dally: 'There's still lots of good in the world. Tell Dally, I don't think he knows.'

characterised by a dynamic use of spatial and musical categories, as opposed to intellectual or literary ones' (1987: 51). Similarly, Christine Gledhill underscores the genre's 'recourse to gestural, visual and musical excess' and its emphasis on 'unpremeditated feeling as an index of moral status and social value' (1987b: 30, 24). I have already discussed the music and score in *The Outsiders* at length, so here I would like to comment on the spatial choices in the film, the 'gestural and visual excesses' that clearly draw upon a melodramatic aesthetic. In addition to his use of Panavision – which, as Burum notes, 'gives you a lot of compositional space' (quoted in 'Staying Gold' 2005) – Coppola's choice of medium, medium close-up, and close-up shots privileges a spatial relationship of closeness and intimacy associated with the melodrama (see Figures 3.8 and 3.9). Indeed, in *The Outsiders*, the characters in the film are 'always in the foreground, never seen in the distance of visual narrative' (Chaillet and Vincent 1984: 95).

Figures 3.8 and 3.9 The close-up as reinforcement of intimacy

Emotion and intimacy are further established through Coppola's repeated use of the two shot. Whereas the shot-reverse-shot is often employed in scenes involving the male Socs and the Greasers, thereby heightening the tension and threat of violence in those scenes, the two shot is frequently used in moments of emotional vulnerability: for example, with Ponyboy and Cherry (see Figure 3.10) and Johnny and Dally (see Figure 3.11). It is also frequently employed in scenes with Ponyboy and Johnny, as Figure 3.9 demonstrates. In each of these scenes, at least one of the characters is revealing something personal or emotional. Johnny cries about the violence in his life and wonders if there's a place 'without Greasers or Socs,' 'some place with just plain ordinary people.' Cherry asks Ponyboy to 'Tell me about your oldest brother,' a question to which Ponyboy responds with an angry outburst: 'He can't stand me. I bet he wishes he could stick me in some

Figures 3.10 and 3.11 The two shot as reinforcement of emotional vulnerability

boys' home or something [...].' Dally desperately tells Johnny to reconsider turning himself in, because 'you get mean in jail.' One of the central purposes of the two shot is 'to show the emotions and reactions of two people in a scene' (Nashville Film Institute no date); it is thus an ideal choice for the genre and for Coppola's heartfelt narrative.

The 'gestural and visual excess' common to melodrama is prevalent in *The Outsiders* as well, seen most clearly in the characters' physical and emotional impulsiveness, and perhaps most significantly, in the amount of crying that occurs in the film. In Chapter 2, I discussed the frequency of crying in Hinton's novel; as a trope, it underscores the characters' youth and vulnerability. Scholars and critics often comment on how Coppola's adaptation remains remarkably faithful to the novel, and I would argue that he does so most extraordinarily in his representations of male emotion on the screen. Both contemporaneous reviews of the film and more recent retrospectives remark on the intensity of emotion in *The Outsiders*. As film critic Sean Burns observes: 'It's striking how vulnerable these kids are, with Coppola emphasizing almost feminine tenderness between them. Even Matt Dillon's swaggering delinquent is perpetually on the verge of tears' (2018). Figure 3.2, for example, shows Dally 'crying, as disoriented as a child, after Johnny's death' (Chaillet and Vincent 1984: 100). Figures 3.12–3.14 likewise illustrate how images of tears and crying are central to the plot and character development of the film. There are no fewer than eight crying scenes in the original version of the film. In *The Complete Novel*, an additional four scenes have been restored, two of which (Pony and Johnny in exile; Soda's monologue about not wanting his brothers to fight) are extended tearful exchanges between the characters that end in emotional embraces. Denis Wood remarks on the many instances of touch and affection between the boys throughout the film, counting 'no less than twenty-eight instances of mutual aid in the film.' As he succinctly puts it, '[t]he camaraderie is everywhere" (1994: 109). The emotiveness of *The Outsiders* at once reinforces its generic identity as a melodrama and sets it apart from other 1980s teen films. While other teen films of the 1980s center on their protagonists' feelings – *Sixteen Candles, The Breakfast Club,* and *Say Anything...* are prime examples – those feelings tend to focus primarily on the desire for love, sex, or acceptance into a social clique. The desire that circulates in *The Outsiders* is of another kind: for safety, a home, a sense of belonging and brotherhood. And that desire is reinforced by the conventions of the genre, by the ways in which form informs and shapes feeling.

The relationship between form and feeling is exemplified in the film's most iconic scene, Ponyboy's recitation of Robert Frost's poem

Figures 3.12–3.14 Gestural and visual excesses define *The Outsiders*

'Nothing Gold Can Stay' (see Figure 3.15). This moment is as pivotal in the movie as it is in Hinton's book; in *The Complete Novel* edition of the film, it even marks the exact halfway point of the movie.

Figure 3.15 Robert Frost, sunsets, and fleeting youth: lush Panavision combines form and feeling

Bookended by lush long shots but dominated primarily by alternating medium close-up and close-up shots, the 'Nothing Gold Can Stay' scene captures the 'unashamed sentimentality of the book' (Cowie 1989: 169). The scene's establishing shot, a long shot of the sunset, clearly parallels scenes from another romantic melodrama, *Gone With the Wind* (Mazer 2018).[5] The relevance of *Gone With the Wind* vis-à-vis *The Outsiders* is twofold. First and foremost, it is the book that Ponyboy reads to Johnny when they are in exile; it keeps them occupied with a story of intrigue and inspiration. Second, as noted in Chapter 2, it is a film that Coppola explicitly identified as an influence on his directorial choices. The end result is a 1980s teen film that mirrors an epic Hollywood classic in look and scope. *Variety's* 1983 review of the film remarks how 'some visual effects of red-drenched sunsets back-dropping the characters strongly evoke similar shots in "GWTW"' ('Review of *The Outsiders*' 1983: 18). More clearly than in any other scene, the cinematography and characterization combine to reinforce the experience of the 'freshness and vitality of youth' (Cowie 1989: 169), the deep emotional bond between Ponyboy and Johnny. Both the poem and the scene, shot so beautifully by cinematographer Steven Burum, represent the ethos of the film as a whole: a visual and emotional narrative privileging the young boys' feelings.

The vulnerability and tenderness between Ponyboy and Johnny in this scene is at once exceptional and representative. It is exceptional because, as Johnny says about his and Pony's appreciation for sunsets, 'I guess we're different, huh?' In this moment, they recognize their kinship with each other: not only as the youngest members of the gang, but also as the ones most desirous of a world outside of class conflict and violence. Yet it is representative, too, because the displays of unaffected innocence and companionship exhibited here between the boys in fact infuse the entirety of the film. They emerge when, on the way to the drive-in, Dally playfully grabs Johnny's head 'with his right arm, bopping it with his left' (Wood 1994: 104), and when Darry tenderly carries Ponyboy from the car to his bed after the fire in Windrixville. They reveal themselves when Two-Bit tells Johnny's abusive mother to 'go straight to hell,' and when Darry screams, 'He's just a kid!' after the police shoot and kill Dally. Such instances remind viewers of the Greasers' hardships, to be sure. But they also remind viewers of their characters' adolescence, their need for play and care, and their protectiveness of each other in the absence of positive adult influences. As Priyanka Bose observes, 'tenderness between young men [...] is the thread that runs throughout the film' (2021).

From another perspective, it is possible to read the film's representation of male camaraderie and intimacy as deeply problematic. In their book *Camera Politica*, Michael Ryan and Douglas Kellner argue that the whole of Coppola's oeuvre, including *The Outsiders*, 'display[s] an inability to come to terms with the crisis of patriarchy initiated by feminism' (1988: 66). They further assert that Coppola's films of the late 70s and early 80s – films in which 'men either live separately from women in all-male groups or else violently reject women' – reveal his investment in 'authoritarian patriarchal ideals' (72, 71). *Time* movie critic Richard Corliss likewise contends that the Greasers' 'ideal world is both a womb and a locker room; no women need apply to this dreamy brother hood' (1983: 78). While Cherry is an important character insofar as she 'inadvertently sets in motion the chain of events that causes several deaths' (Macnab 2021), she is also *exactly that*: the person who could be seen as responsible in some way for fueling the fire between the Socs and the Greasers. Her testimony in the courtroom scene – a scene added back into the film in *The Complete Novel* version of the movie, and ending with a line that does not appear in the novel – makes this point even clearer: 'I could have made it simpler for the fight not to have happened in the first place.' I admit to feeling discomfort when hearing this line, as it seems to position Cherry as a scapegoat. At the same time, I disagree with assessments of the film that identify it as patriarchal or anti-feminist. The absence of women alone does not a patriarchal text make. Narrative content matters, too, and what *The Outsiders* offers is a narrative built around demonstrative, authentic relationships among young boys – relationships in which their vulnerability is an asset, not a detriment. In this way it runs counter to most conventional representations of adolescent masculinity of the era. As Sheila Johnston affirms in her review of the film, this is a rare representation indeed: 'it is encouraging to find a youth movie that views its rites of passage in loftier terms than simply getting laid' (1983). It is so rare that reviews of the film could not help but comment on it, and not in positive terms.

Conclusion: Genre and Gender

In both reviews of the film and studies of Coppola's work, there has been ample commentary – most of it negative – on the emotional and visual excesses of *The Outsiders.* Troubled by what they deemed unrealistic or even uncomfortable representations of 'adolescent males repeatedly crying and expressing affection for each other' (Chown 1988: 165), critics often dismiss *The Outsiders* as overwrought pablum. Reviews of the film, which I discuss at greater length in the next chapter, almost unanimously judged the film as 'silly, unpretentious, and unambitious' (Lewis 1995: 102). Most Coppola scholars agree with this assessment. Jon Lewis further asserts that *The Outsiders* is 'Coppola's least original and least satisfying film' (100), and Jeffrey Chown describes the film as an 'unpretentious stylistic exercise, not an example of auteur cinema' (1988: 166). Peter Cowie warns that '[t]he borderline between the cute and the cloying is a slender one' (1989: 169), and according to most critics, *The Outsiders* walks that line too uneasily. Interestingly, they see the story of *The Outsiders* and the emotional import Coppola gave to it as beneath him, proof of his fall as a director. As *Newsweek* film critic David Ansen pointedly asked in his review of the film: 'Who would have expected a teary teen soap opera from the maker of "The Godfather" and "Apocalypse Now?"' (1983: 74).

I contend that these critiques of the film are deeply rooted in the relationship between genre and gender. Sue Harper observes how melodrama is most often viewed by film scholars and critics as

> the domain of the feminine, because it was mainly attended by female audiences. Melodrama's lack of critical status can be attributed to this popular/feminine bias. Its concentration on taboo, ritual, rage and desire – all expressed without restraint – meant that most male critics, who preferred emotions to be spoken *sotto voce*, found melodrama to be tasteless.
>
> (no date)

Melodrama addresses the realm of the feminine and the domestic – realms historically seen as frivolous and insignificant in comparison to the power and public influence of the masculine. Coppola chooses this genre to tell the story of *boys*, not girls, yet as I discussed above, he retains the genre's attachment to feeling, as well as some of its other key components. In the eyes of some critics, then, he feminizes the male leads and thereby cheapens the film. At the heart of most critiques of *The Outsiders* is Coppola's foregrounding of emotion 'expressed without restraint.' It is seen as a movie that feels *too much*, and as such, is embarrassing in its earnestness. Jeffrey Chown asserts that 'fourteen-year-old males [in the film] act emotionally very much like stereotypical fourteen-year-old females, although the outward trappings of fist fights, interest in cars, and athletics *seems* very masculine' (1988: 165, italics added). Richard Corliss likewise casts doubt on the masculinity of the boys and in doing so, expresses his disdain for the film: 'Their camaraderie is familial, embracing, unself-consciously homoerotic. Left to their better selves, they can easily go all moony over sunsets, quote great swatches of Robert Frost verse, or fall innocently asleep in each other's arms' (1983: 78). David Ansen marvels at the naïveté of the film, at once recognizing and critiquing the conventions of the melodramatic film: 'these boys cry, fight, run from the law and speechify not according to the laws of human nature but the dictates of movie history' (1983: 74). Finally, Armand White dismissingly describes how the film 'treated a boy's attraction to his tender-hearted brothers and buddies as a rite of ecstasy, and thus threw the whole issue of teen heroism into the shadows of latent homosexuality' (1985: 10).[6]

In her book *Lost Angels: Psychoanalysis and Cinema*, Vicky Lebeau asserts that an 'overly familiar link between a homo-eroticized form of social identification and a repudiation of femininity runs through reviews of *The Outsiders*' (1995: 94). The undercurrent of homophobia and sexism that runs through such criticism underscores the ways in which genre and gender are inextricably linked. With its male characters in a traditionally female genre, *The Outsiders* defies expectations of gender. If *The Outsiders* were about a female gang instead of a male gang, and if the film's director had not been Coppola, the contemporary criticism of the film perhaps would not have been quite so unforgiving. In a more recent re-evaluation of the film, *New York Times* film critic Manohla Dargis appreciates the movie for its representation of 'tender male beauty' and notes that while 'physical closeness between straight male characters is nearly absent from our screens,' *The Outsiders* does not shy away from such displays of affection (2005). It also resists many of the standard tropes of the other genre to which it belongs: the teen film. Frances Smith identifies how a 'substantial proportion of Hollywood teen movies end in an idealized heterosexual romance'

(2017: 3). *The Outsiders* does not. In myriad ways, then, Coppola's film stands apart in the annals of 1980s teen films.

A formal analysis of Coppola's *The Outsiders* emphasizes how the representation of intense feelings – feelings usually associated with adolescence – is achieved through the movie's cinematography, composition, and characterization. It also reveals how unusual it is for a teen film of the 1980s to locate that representation in young men. The affect within the film expanded well beyond the four walls of the screen. The pre-release hype for the movie was directed at an audience known for their emotions: pre-teen and adolescent girls. In juxtaposition to the negative responses from film critics whose dominant feelings about *The Outsiders* were those of disappointment and contempt, the ecstatic reporting on the film in teen magazines created a remarkable buzz around *The Outsiders* well before its release. In Chapter 4, I examine these two discourses side by side so as to reveal the conflicting narratives about the film: on the one hand, a movie that marked the continuing failure of a once-famed auteur, and on the other hand, a film that stirred the hearts of so many adolescents that their emotional response guaranteed its box-office success. As it turned out, the 'teary teen soap opera' that David Ansen scorned was the very genre that young fans in the early 1980s wanted to see.

Notes

1 Though Coppola's film effectively represents the poverty in which the Greasers live and the class tensions that define their existence, its treatment of the topic is somewhat muted when compared to Hinton's text, which gives us access to Ponyboy's thoughts about class inequality and injustice across the novel.

2 Shary positions both *The Outsiders* and *Rumble Fish* as contributing to 'the increasing legitimacy of the youth film genre during that decade' (2014: 147). Susannah Gora likewise observes how the script of *The Outsiders* 'offered many meaty roles for young people, something that felt new and different' (2010: 22).

3 Two other teen films of the era that clearly nod to *Rebel Without a Cause* as influence and inspiration are *Heathers* (Lehmann, 1989) and *Pump Up the Volume* (Moyle, 1990).

4 While it could be argued that melodrama is a genre 'that has developed without any true sense of origin, continuity or style' (Merritt 1983: 31), or that it is 'the fundamental mode of popular American moving pictures' (Williams 1998: 42), most critics agree that specific emotions, plots, and tropes are common to the melodrama. For further discussion of the complexities of the genre, see Christine Gledhill's landmark collection *Home is Where the Heart Is: Studies in Melodrama and the Woman's Film* (1987a). John Mercer and Martin Shingler's *Melodrama: Genre, Style, Sensibility* (2004) also provides an excellent overview of the various debates among scholars of the genre.

5 This image is repeated in the final on-screen exchange between Ponyboy and Cherry, when he asks her if she can see the sunset from the south side.

6 Coppola scholar Gene D. Phillips pushes back on such homoerotic readings of the film, arguing that

> [t]hose critics who have inferred a hint of homosexuality in this film misconstrue the value that Coppola places on male companionship in his movies [...] Ponyboy and Johnny have not yet experienced a deep relationship in their lives. Consequently, they are experiencing in their friendship a relationship that is fulfilling for them on an emotional level that has nothing to do with sex.
>
> (2004: 210)

Though I absolutely recognize how the film can be read as containing potentially homoerotic elements and relationships, I generally agree with Phillips. In my estimation, the instances of affection are not sexual but familial; in particular, Ponyboy and Johnny are essentially still children and are played by Howell and Macchio as such, so I contend that their need to confide in and physically hold each other stems from a desire for comfort and stability, not sex.

4 'Matt, Ralph, & Tom Will Make You Cry'

The Critics, the Fans, and the Reception of *The Outsiders*

From the date that librarian Jo Ellen Misakian sent the letter on behalf of her students to Francis Ford Coppola – 21 March 1980 – to the date that *The Outsiders* was finally released in U.S. theaters on 25 March 1983, three full years had passed. In that time, the critical curiosity and marketing hype around the film grew from a low hum to a feverish buzz. The anticipation over the release of the film must be understood within three distinct but interrelated contexts. The first, as noted briefly in Chapter 2, is that of the director and his oeuvre. In the wake of the critical and box office failure of *One from the Heart*, Coppola needed to produce a movie that proved he still had it as a director, *and* that proved he could make a movie within a budget – in this case, a small, strict budget of $10 million, a paltry sum compared to what Coppola had spent on *Apocalypse Now* ($31 million) and *One From the Heart* ($27 million) (Phillips 2004: 206, 155, 197). The second context is the fan base of the novel. Since its publication in 1967, *The Outsiders* had been taught in U.S. middle and high schools on a continual basis, selling 4 million copies by the time Coppola took on the project (Corliss 1983: 78).[1] Its fans – like the students who signed Misakian's letter, and like me, an adolescent reader who fell in love with the novel – were loyal to the book and excited to see it turned into a movie. As such, in the United States, the movie had a built-in fan base, a 'ready-made audience[]' (Schumacher 1999: 316). Finally, there is the specific historic and cultural moment at which the film appeared. Teen films were gaining audiences in the 1980s, and equally significant, so were their stars. The youth cinema that preceded *The Outsiders* typically featured casts of relatively unknown actors: *Fast Times at Ridgemont High,* for example, is notable for starting the careers of many then-unknown players, including Sean Penn, Jennifer Jason Leigh, Phoebe Cates, and Judge Reinhold. But no teen film in the early 1980s

DOI: 10.4324/9781003228783-5

featured a cast comprised almost exclusively of young men, most of them also unknowns and some of whom would later become part of the infamous 'Brat Pack.'[2] This casting meant that in the United States, *The Outsiders* attracted a following unlike any other early '80s teen film: readers of teen magazines. And these readers were passionate about *The Outsiders*, fanatics in the truest sense of the word.

In one corner, the fans of Hinton's book and devoted readers of teen magazines. In the other corner, the critics, who almost uniformly dismissed the film as disappointing and irrelevant. Most fascinating about this match is the diametrically opposed responses to *The Outsiders*: the frenzied embrace by the young viewers of the movie and the drumming by the critics. In this chapter, I explore these contradictory dynamics. Whereas one group expressed derision toward the film's sentimentality and its representation of the young men as objects of desire, the other group celebrated those very same things. Ultimately, I will argue that the critics' disdain toward both youth culture and conventionally feminine pursuits informed their negative evaluations of the film. These negative appraisals had little effect on its intended audience, of course. To be sure, '*The Outsiders* was embraced by a youth audience' (Lewis 2016: 6), and they drove the movie's box office earnings. The passion and loyalty of the film's original audiences help to explain its ongoing cult following, which I explore in Chapter 5.

'Mere Doggerel': Film Critics Respond to *The Outsiders*

Though *The Outsiders* was a moderate box-office success, grossing $33.7 million (Godfrey 2021: 101), it was not a critical success by any stretch of the imagination. On the contrary, most critics saw it as the nail in the coffin for Coppola, signaling the end of his decade-long run as one of the premier auteurs of Hollywood cinema. They agreed that the film was a significant step down for Coppola in terms of content and theme. Coppola biographers and scholars discuss the troubled reception of the film in various ways. Schumacher, for example, notes how the critics 'thumb[ed] their noses at the story [...] their appraisals saturated in the kind of cynicism and regret that had inspired S.E. Hinton to write her novel' (1999: 323). Jon Lewis describes the reviews as 'scathing,' noting that the movie received 'only one favorable notice (from Joseph Gelmis at *Newsday*) out of eleven from the New York critics' (1995: 101). According to Coppola's biographers, the critics 'mocked Coppola for having chosen such a simple, if not trite, story' (Chaillet and Vincent 1984: 98) and 'chastised Coppola for making such a silly, unpretentious, and unambitious little film' (Lewis 1995: 102). Surveying the reviews, Gene D. Phillips describes how most critics concluded that the film was a 'minor melodrama unworthy of Coppola's directorial talents' (2004: 212).

These summaries are not exaggerations. On the whole, the reaction among film critics was not kind.[3] In 'Playing Tough, Going Nowhere,' longtime *Time* movie reviewer Richard Corliss outlined the landscape on which Coppola's film was being released: 'After the life-or-death marketing of *Apocalypse Now* and *One from the Heart*, it is refreshing to come upon a Coppola film that is, bless it, only a movie.' He then delivered his assessment of it: 'Alas, *The Outsiders* is not quite a good one [...] the picture never manages to reach the peaks of satisfying Hollywood melodrama' (1983: 78). David Denby of *New York* magazine was harsher in his estimation of the film. Disparaging the movie for its 'outright sentimentality,' he claimed that *The Outsiders* is 'heartfelt, utterly humorless, and shockingly banal,' an 'overblown, inauthentic movie, and a dull one too' (1983: 73). Jeffrey Wells, in *Film Journal International*, agreed: 'Muddled, incoherent and garishly sentimental, this is the sort of film that seems determined to screw itself up, despite every chance to do otherwise' (1983: 35). Writing for *Rolling Stone*, Michael Sragow was no kinder: 'Coppola has aimed for the poetry of youth and achieved mere doggerel' (1983: 55).

While it could be argued that these reviews legitimately highlight the flaws and shortcomings of the film, they also must be understood within the context of the director's oeuvre. What every one of them has in common is the feeling of deep dissatisfaction in Coppola's directing, the sense that the famed auteur responsible for two of the most impactful films of the 1970s had lost his magic touch. Kenneth Turan perhaps best summed up the feeling among critics at the time of the film's release:

> *The Outsiders* is a serious disappointment – one more backward step in what has become the saddest decline in American film [...] there is no sense of energy or excitement, no pace to the various scenes, not the barest sign that the director is the same man who brought such an alive, bravura sensibility to the *Godfather* films [...] What *The Outsiders* shows is that Coppola is either too involved, too forgetful, or too unnerved by the troubles his past films have endured to be able to function at the level of assurance that made his reputation.
>
> (1983: 120, 121)

Though hard on Coppola, Turan's review is actually generous compared to others, which are at turns impatient, excoriating, and hostile. Where has the great auteur gone? they wonder. Coppola's 'greatness' – or rather, its marked absence – is the through line in these reviews. 'The movie is a frightening failure: One searches in vain for signs of Coppola's greatness' (1983: 73), declared Denby. Describing *The Outsiders* as 'a stylistic exercise,' Roger Ebert proclaimed that the 'man who made the "Godfather" pictures and "Apocalypse Now" is a great director. He ought to reserve these exercises for the rehearsal halls of his fancy and get back to making movies' (1983b). Their disappointment led some critics to chastise Coppola – and, in condescending terms like those of Ebert, to offer him both career and personal advice. In the *San Francisco Chronicle*, for example, Peter Stack mused how 'Coppola cannot seem to set aside his native urge to fashion movies into epics. Perhaps he should be required to re-read the lyrics of Robert Frost, whose largest visions were given to us in plain terms, the way the heart always speaks' (1983: 62). Rita Kemply of the *Washington Post* concurred, declaring that *The Outsiders* is 'silly filmmaking, the sort of thing you don't expect from a master like Coppola, who seems to be stuck in a second childhood. Please, please, get it worked out, Mr. Coppola, and grow back up' (1983). Summing up the judgments of Coppola's vision, Vincent Canby offered the following sardonic observation about the director: '"Outsiders," which, coming on the heels, so to speak, of "One From the Heart," leads one to suspect that Mr. Coppola is no longer with us, but up with his entourage observing the world from a space platform' (1983: 18).

Why would a great director take on a project about kids and so clearly for kids, and why would he do so with such seriousness and earnestness? Canby and the like struggled with the enigma of Coppola's choices. Recognizing the film as both a teen movie and a melodrama, the critics expressed their disdain accordingly. Canby called *The Outsiders* 'a melodramatic kid-film with the narrative complexity of "The Three Bears" and a high body count' (1983: 18). Denby dismissively labelled the film as 'a true kids' movie (13-year-olds should love it)' (1983: 73). Most of these dismissals of the film are rooted in the opinion that the material was at once beneath Coppola and misguidedly elevated by him. Their critique, then, was inextricably linked to the film's content, genre, and audience. An epic movie about adult men embroiled in the mafia? Genius filmmaking. A melodrama about parentless teenagers who struggle to find their place in the world? Doggerel. As Jon Lewis concludes: '*The Outsiders* had improved [Coppola's] position in the industry at the expense of his standing as an *auteur* and as an artist' (1995: 103).

It is crucial to recognize, however, just how unconventional Coppola's approach to making *The Outsiders* was at the time. The '80s Hollywood teen film was just taking off, and most of the time its success was guaranteed by its comedic underpinnings. Coppola, by contrast, was tackling serious, even melancholy, youth content. In choosing to frame the film as a melodrama, he was validating the depth and complexity of kids' feelings. As he said in an interview at the time of the film's release: 'It appealed to me that kids could see *Outsiders* as a lavish, big feeling epic about kids' (quoted in Thomson and Gray 1983: 65). The end result was a serious, important film *for them.*[4] This is perhaps most poignantly captured in 'A Boy's View of "Outsiders,"' (1983) an editorial published in the *Los Angeles Times* written by 12-year-old Todd Camhe. In his opening line, he proclaimed, '*The Outsiders* is the first movie that's just about kids and their problems. I think that's important' (1983). Camhe was speaking on behalf of the youth audience of *The Outsiders* who saw themselves or their friends reflected in the film – and who did not understand the critical drumming the film took. 'Most of the critics are looking at the kids in the movie as characters with problems,' said Camhe, 'but they don't really identify with them because they don't care' (ibid.).

The kids who saw the movie, however, *did* care – and felt the characters' anguish deeply. Indeed, those kids' interest in and enthusiasm for *The Outsiders* contributed to its box-office success; it grossed $5 million dollars in its opening weekend (the second highest-grossing film of the week of 25-31 March 1983, edged out of first place by the raunchy teen comedy *Spring Break*), and over $30 million dollars in its forty-week theater run ('Domestic Grosses' 2022). Lewis notes how '*The Outsiders* remained on *Variety's* top fifty list for almost three months. By the time its first run was over it proved to be Coppola's most successful outing in almost five years' (1995: 101-2). Warner Bros. capitalized on the popular success of the film: 'they defined *The Outsiders* as an event film, or at least as a picture film audiences (as opposed to critics) seemed to like' (101). Well before the movie's release, however, the studio had been priming audiences through its marketing plan, one in which they shared information about *The Outsiders* 'to a select public – specifically, young people. Warner Bros. and Zoetrope concentrated on the specialized magazines and television programs devoted to teenagers. Warner Bros. wanted to market *The Outsiders* as a film for the younger generation' (Chaillet and Vincent 1984: 97). They did so, quite successfully. The critics underestimated the loyalty and interest of U.S. teenage moviegoers – the burgeoning (mostly female) fan base being built off the popularity of the book and heightened by the fandom being whipped up by teen magazines. It is in these magazines that the film found its most enthusiastic and welcome marketing home.

'Be Part of the Most Exciting New Movie for Teens!': Marketing to the Female Teen Audience

> This is the story of how a very special movie got made. It stars some of the people you love best and it introduces others you're going to love just as much. It's *16*'s very own exclusive behind-the-scenes series of what went on while the cameras were rolling and what happened when it wasn't! *The Outsiders* – on camera and off – is a story for you.
>
> ('The Making of *The Outsiders* Part 1' 1982: 6)

Well before its actual release date of 25 March 1983, *The Outsiders* was deeply embedded in the consciousness of thousands of pre-teen and teenage girls in the United States. I know because I was one of them. For months leading up to the film's debut, I devoured any news of the movie that I could get my hands on, and for me that news came in the form of my source for all pop culture knowledge: teen magazines. While '[m]agazines targeting the teenage girl market have been around in the United States since 1944 when *Seventeen* magazine published its first issue,' the market truly exploded in the late 1950s-early to mid-1960s with the establishment of *16* (founded in 1957), *Tiger Beat* (founded in 1965), and *Teen Beat* (founded in 1967) (Shelton no date). During my pre-adolescent and adolescent years in the late 1970s-early 1980s, these titles dominated the market. They were building off their success in prior decades, when they capitalized on the fan frenzy around Elvis Presley, the Beatles, the Monkees, Bobby Sherman, David Cassidy, the Osmonds, and Leif Garrett, among others (the last of whom, of course, would go on to play Bob Sheldon in *The Outsiders*). And they targeted a very specific demographic: girls with disposable income from their parents. Jacob Shelton explains how as early as the 1950s, marketers seized the opportunity to profit from this demographic: 'If these young girls could afford to buy 45s and albums and concert tickets, and had a limitless attention-span when it came to their favorite male actors and musicians, surely they'd buy magazines hyping these same subjects. And these young female fans did just that, as expected. Teen magazines were big business, and competition was intense' (ibid.).[5]

Shelton's description of the demographic as 'young girls' accurately captures the primary readership of these magazines. Children's literature scholar Perry Nodelman observes that although the titles of these magazines 'speak of youth,' the readers 'are not often teenagers: most are ten or eleven or twelve' (1986: 104). Nodelman's assertion is certainly borne out in my own experience. I began my weekly bike-ride to the grocery store for these magazines at a very young age: around seven or eight, when I became obsessed with my first teen idol crush, Shaun Cassidy. I remained an avid reader of them until the age of 14, when I started high school and switched to the more mature version of the teen magazine, *Seventeen*. Based on the scant research available on these magazines – research which discusses either their publication history or their typically 'sexy but safe' representation of male teen idols (which I explore further below) – I contend that girls between the ages of nine and 14 were the target demographic. Most obvious to anyone familiar with these magazines, this audience was also assumed to be heterosexual, and thus the ways in which the young boys (and men) are presented is geared toward the formation of pre-adolescent and adolescent desire. As such, the images and copy in these magazines was typically devoid of any explicit sexual content but still offered 'a safe means of expressing sexual interest for beginners' (107). The magazines I explore in this section at once present the actors in *The Outsiders* as objects of desire and hype the movie itself as an event unparalleled by any other person or occasion featured on their pages. As early as May 1982, the marketing machine for Coppola's film was in action, galvanizing readers for the then-planned October distribution of the movie.

Of all the teen magazines, only one made *The Outsiders* front and center for well over a year: *16*. According to the website *Nostalgia Central*, in the U.S. periodical market *16* 'set the standard for all teen magazines' ('16 Magazine'); its writing, photos, and features were decidedly more sophisticated than those of its competitors. The magazine also 'maintained a consistent editorial tone that reflected editor Gloria Stavers's respect for, and commitment to, the emotional concerns of her readership' (Nash 2003: 142). For almost a full year, *16* offered full-court press coverage of the movie, hyping it initially via the two male stars whom they'd already been covering in months prior: Matt Dillon and Ralph Macchio. By the third month of promotion, the editors added C. Thomas Howell to the mix, ultimately identifying him, Macchio, and Dillon as the 'three "stars" of the movie' ('The Making of *The Outsiders* Part 6' 1983: 7). At the same time that the magazine piqued its readers' interest in the film via these actors it also encouraged an anticipatory emotional investment in *The Outsiders*, going so far as to suggest that 'It Just *May* Be The Most Memorable Movie Event Of Your Life!' ('*The Outsiders* Is Coming!' 1982: 17, italics in original).

Foremost among the reasons for this hyperbolic claim is the film's exclusive focus – in terms of its source material, its plot, and its performers – on a youth audience:

> Take one book written *for* teenagers, *by* a 17-year-old that tells a powerful and gripping story *from* a young person's point of view – now, mix that with a half dozen (or so) major young stars of today and put it all up on the silver screen. What have you got? You've got a can't-miss blockbuster of a movie – that you're going to see and cherish again and again. You've got *The Outsiders.*
>
> ('*The Outsiders* Is Coming!' 1982: 17, italics in original)

Recognizing the uniqueness of *The Outsiders* in the burgeoning genre of youth cinema in the early 1980s, *16* promised to provide all the 'exclusive' news it could for its loyal readers. Over the course of a year, it delivered on its promise. Worth noting is that the date on each issue of *16* is actually two months ahead of its real-time distribution, which means that '*The Outsiders* is Coming!' actually made its way to readers in May 1982, well in advance of the initially scheduled October 1982 release date. What ended up happening as a result of the film's continually delayed debut, however, was that the promotional articles and posters in *16* were stretched out for over a year. From its July 1982 issue (published in May 1982) to its August 1983 issue (published in June 1983), *16* featured stories on *The Outsiders* every single month, with no fewer than an annual total of 60 pages on the individual stars, the entire cast, and/or the film, as well as multiple color pinups of Dillon, Macchio, and Howell.

Nodelman observes how most male celebrities featured in teen magazines are shaped to fit a very specific persona for the young female audience: as 'sensitive souls who couldn't hurt anyone' (1986: 110). He further explains how '[t]hese are safe fantasy lovers [...] a boy this gentle, this kind, is no threat' (ibid.). This formula is borne out in the stories and images of the cast of *The Outsiders*. *16*'s coverage of Dillon, Macchio, and Howell plays to the features of the teen idol that Nodelman identifies, providing young girls with a way to explore their nascent (hetero)sexual desire. The star most frequently presented as the object of desire was Matt Dillon. Dillon had been on the teen magazine radar due to his work in *Over the Edge* (Kaplan, 1980),

My Bodyguard (Bill, 1981), and *Little Darlings* (Maxwell, 1981) and, as *16* observed, was 'the most well-known of the cast' ('The Making of *The Outsiders* Part 1' 1982: 6).[6] More importantly, he was considered the most alluring because of the parallels between his version of movie-star cool and that of Dallas Winston. The articles often proclaim that Dally is 'the most important part he's played so far' and *The Outsiders* is 'the *only* book [Dillon] ever daydreamed about as a movie' ('*The Outsiders* is Coming!' 1982: 18, italics in original). In an article entitled 'Matt Dillon's Private Life!' readers learn several tidbits about Dillon, including that while he was not considered a '"hood" in school, Matt did live up to his tough guy reputation – it wasn't unlikely to find him in a fight' (1983: 10) and that he has 'taken to wearing an earring in his left ear' (11). The earring – a significant sign of rebellion for straight men in the early 1980s – marks him as daring and defiant, like Dally. At the same time, the bad-boy appeal of Dillon is often tempered by reminders of his thoughtful, harmless nature. A feature article assures readers that

> whatever he did – including getting into scuffles – never qualified him for a "bad boy" tag [...] and if he did go through a tough, macho period, he never hurt anyone. And besides, if you really knew him well, you could probably dig beneath that rough exterior and find a pretty good person there.
>
> ('Matt Dillon: Don't Believe ALL You Read!' 1983: 28)

16 capitalizes on Dillon's stardom by presenting him as a 'pretty good person' in a 'foxy' package: a celebrity with whom young girls can feel at ease in their adolescent longing. That he is featured as a pinup in virtually every issue underscores his availability as a 'Street Smart 'N Sexy' object of desire (June 1983 cover) (see Figure 4.1).[7]

In contrast to Dillon, Macchio and Howell are not presented as good guys in bad boy's clothing. '[M]ore sensitive in appearance' and therefore even less threatening (Nodelman 1986: 105), they represent objects of romance rather than lust. Of the two, Macchio is featured more prominently across the yearlong span of promotional articles (though by the March 1983 issue, Howell had taken top billing over him). In 1982, Macchio had not yet broken into successful mainstream films; his lone film role to date was in *MAD Magazine's Up the Academy* (Downey Sr.) released in 1980, but was better known to readers of *16* for playing Jeremy Andretti in the 1980-81 season of the U.S. hit television series *Eight is Enough* (ABC, 1977-81). Across the year of *Outsiders* coverage, young fans learn that Macchio is perhaps the most serious of all the

Figure 4.1 Matt Dillon is 'Street Smart 'N Sexy,' an object of lust and desire

actors in the film. Like Dillon, he desperately wanted a part in the film for two reasons: because 'he found a lot of depth to Johnny' ('The Making of *The Outsiders* Part 4' 1982: 15) and because 'the movie is being directed by one of the most respected and well-known talents around – Francis Ford Coppola' ('*The Outsiders* is Coming!' 1982: 18). And *16* repeatedly assures readers that Macchio is a perfect choice for Johnny because his 'big brown eyes' reflect Johnny's 'fear and innocence' (ibid.). But ambition and puppy-dog eyes are not Macchio's only admirable qualities. Readers learn that Macchio loves his family, Bruce Springsteen and Robert DeNiro ('Ralph Macchio: What Turns Him On … & Off!' 1983: 64-5) and that he hates 'all the phoniness and game playing that's so rampant in Hollywood' ('The Making of *The Outsiders* Part 6' 1983: 8). Adding to his appeal as an attractive, down-to-earth young man, readers learn that 'Ralph is the kind of guy who needs to be friends with a girl before the romantic feelings come' (9). The embodiment of 'gentle vulnerability' (Nodelman 1986: 110), Macchio is truly adorable: a celebrity to admire and safely desire (see Figure 4.2).

Figure 4.2 Ralph Macchio, the embodiment of 'gentle vulnerability'

Finally, there is C. Thomas Howell, who like Macchio is also presented as 'singularly unaggressive' (Nodelman 1986: 111). The youngest member of the cast, he is closest in age to readers of *16* and thus often characterized as innocent and down-to-earth (see Figure 4.3). A 'brown-eyed babe' who is as 'warm and fun-loving a teen as you'll ever meet' ('The Making of *The Outsiders* Part 3' 1982: 31), Howell plays 'one of the most magnetic and irresistible screen characters you'll ever meet' ('The Making of *The Outsiders* Part 1' 1982: 7). Like Dillon and Macchio, he 'knew he wanted the role of shy, sensitive Greaser, "Pony"' and worked hard to earn it (ibid.). He is also regularly described as unique for several reasons: his father was a stuntman; his parents divorced when he was two years old; he grew up both in California and in Colorado; and he was tutored for most of his childhood ('Tommy Howell: The Most … ' 1983: 26-7). Tommy is, per the title of one article, 'The Most Unusual Boy You've Ever Met!' (26), and in this way he embodies a different fantasy than those represented by Dillon and Macchio. As more of a peer than an adult male, Howell could be seen by female readers as occupying a different realm

Figure 4.3 C. Thomas Howell, a 'warm and fun-loving teen'

than the others: one 'encouraging girls to see male idols allies, equals, and companions, not merely love objects to be worshiped or "caught"' (Nash 2003: 143). Above all, like so many of his peers, Howell just wants to be accepted. As he expresses in one of his 'messages' to readers: 'I had no idea that you'd take the *Outsiders* to heart so, and that you'd like me – I was *hoping* for it, I thank you for making it happen!' ('*Outsiders* Review! What You Thought! What The Stars Felt! What The Critics Said!' 1983: 5, italics in original).

The varied representations of Dillon, Macchio, and Howell all underscore how *16* invited girls to desire not only physical attractiveness but also particular personality traits in these celebrities: gentleness, a commitment to family, a strong work ethic, and individuality. In doing so, the magazine tapped into both the erotic and the affective components of attraction. It further encouraged a loyal and passionately invested fan following for *The Outsiders* by positioning readers as 'insiders' on knowledge about the film.[8] The magazine established this strategy in its very first article on *The Outsiders*:

> While the film is still being made as you're reading this and probably won't be ready for you to see until (at the *earliest*) this fall, *16* is going to keep you very much involved with the *inside track*. Matt, Ralph and friends assembled in mid-March in Tulsa, Oklahoma for preliminary work and began the actual shooting in early April. What they did when they *weren't* working, *who* became friendly with *whom* and all sorts of behind-the-scenes, hijinks will be ready for you to find out about in upcoming issues of *16*!
>
> ('*The Outsiders* is Coming!' 1982: 18, italics in original)

Throughout the year leading up to the film's release, *16* continually reminds its readers that '*The Outsiders* boys want you to be an insider!' ('The Making of *The Outsiders* Part 1' 1982: 9) and that '[i]f you're a regular *16* reader, you've been following this fascinating series and learning first hand what it's like to make a movie – not *any* movie, mind you, but one with the most fabulous cast assembled anywhere!' ('The Making of *The Outsiders* Part 3' 1982: 30, italics in original). In a 'Fact File' article on Tommy Howell, readers are told that while his full name is C. Thomas Howell, 'you can call him: Tommy – because *you're* a friend' ('Tommy Howell Fact File!' 1983: 30, italics in original). In a list of Ralph's 'loves' and 'hates,' readers learn that Macchio 'hates the fact that he hasn't met you. But he never loses hope that maybe someday he will! (So don't you ever lose it either!)' ('Ralph Macchio …' 1983: 65). In an article responding to mainstream media reports that Matt is a 'bad boy,' *16* reminds readers that 'not everyone knows Matt personally the way you do – because you've been reading about him for many happy moons' ('Matt Dillon: Don't Believe ALL You Read!' 1983: 28, 29). Finally, in the December 1982 issue, the entire cast is featured on the cover, the copy of which offers readers a 'Sneak Peek' of the film and promises to give them 'Your Private Scrapbook!' of the stars (see Figure 4.4).[9]

Well ahead of the film's debut, *16*'s readers were in the know about the film and its stars, and the enthusiasm the magazine conveyed through its coverage was contagious. Teen girls who followed the 'news' on *The Outsiders* were more than ready for the movie to hit the big screens, and when it did, they filled the theaters.

Gender, Desire, and Contempt

The tensions between the critics' scorn and the female teen fans' embrace of *The Outsiders* is noteworthy in terms of what it tells us about

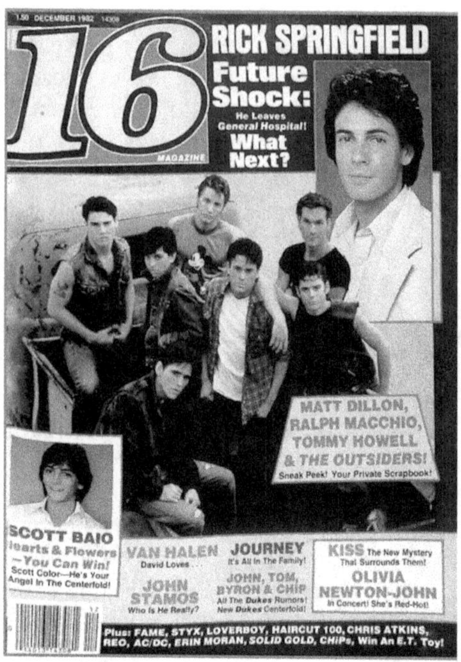

Figure 4.4 Loyal *Outsiders* fans are promised a 'sneak peek' and a 'private scrapbook' of the movie

gendered expectations of film. In Chapter 3 I briefly discussed how the film's generic qualities and lavish cinematography elicited the critics' disapproval. Here, I want to further examine how this disapproval is deeply gendered, sexist, and homophobic. Ilana Nash asserts that '[f]ilms, radio and television programs, newspapers, magazines, and every other form of mass cultural discourse over the last seventy years have constructed young teenage girls as silly, hyperbolic creatures' (2003: 148), and this sentiment is borne out in evaluations of the film. The title of David Ansen's review in *Newsweek* says it all: 'Coppola Courts the Kiddies.' The 'kiddies' he primarily courts are, of course, girls, and other reviews of the movie note this with condescension. Writing in *Sight and Sound,* Gilbert Adair characterizes the movie as 'a melodrama made specifically for the attention of teenagers, a real two-handkerchief (or maybe two-sleeve) weepie' (1983). As noted in Chapter 3, the 'weepie' is a traditionally female film form; in naming the film as such, Adair genders it as well. Arthur

Bell, in his scathing review in the *Village Voice* entitled 'One From the Crotch,' contemptuously describes how '*The Outsiders* is crammed with the darlings of *Sixteen* magazine' (1983: 53), and how during the filming, '[e]ach day, hordes of horny girls would appear at the location site. They waited outside the Excelsior Hotel every night, yelling their dopey little mouths off for their fave rave' (ibid.). Stupid, emotional, and hormonal, the girls waiting for a glimpse of Matt Dillon or any of his co-stars are subjects of mockery. By extension, the film is as well.

Perhaps unwittingly, Bell's description of the star-crazed female fans captured a key component of their behavior: they were 'horny,' sexual beings whose desire was not only romantic but also carnal. That Coppola's film acknowledges and plays to heterosexual female desire is noteworthy. In her superb essay 'Incipient Female Gazing at *The Outsiders*' (2020), Blue Profitt offers a compelling reading of how Coppola's film gave 'young women the opportunity to train their gazes' on objects of desire: Dillon, Howell, Macchio, and the rest of the gang. 'As a film that lays the male figure physically and emotionally bare,' Profitt argues, '*The Outsiders* is a narrative where girls in the audience may be encouraged to do the gazing' (ibid.). While there are several moments in the film that speak directly to the desiring female gaze, two in particular stand out. The first, discussed by Profitt, is when Dally takes Ponyboy and Johnny under his wing to prepare them for their exile. Profitt contends that in this scene and others with Dillon, 'the composition of Dally's body may cater to an incipient female gaze because the framing suggests *potential* for sexual activity without revealing 'too much' of his body all at once' (ibid., italics in original) (see Figure 4.5). As is obvious in the screenshot, Dally's body is what we are meant to look at – and potentially desire. The second, and perhaps most famous insofar as it has elicited the most squeals of delight from female audiences, is Sodapop's shower scene (see Figure 4.6). In these scenes and others, 'the movie positions male bodies as age-appropriate spectacles' for young heterosexual female viewers (Profitt 2020). In doing so, it displaces the dominant male gaze of both the camera and the spectator as described by Laura Mulvey in 'Visual Pleasure in Narrative Cinema' (1999).

This aspect of *The Outsiders* elicits expressions of discomfort from some critics. The way they work through their discomfort is instructive. Take, for example, the title of David Denby's review of the film: 'Romance for Boys' (1983). It gestures toward both the audience of *The Outsiders* (boys, or young people in general) and the potentially homoerotic undertones of the film – and his implied disapproval of both. He complains that as 'a tough, older boy, Matt

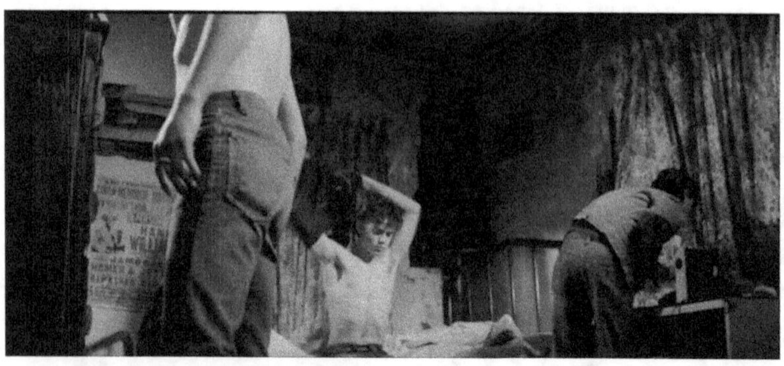

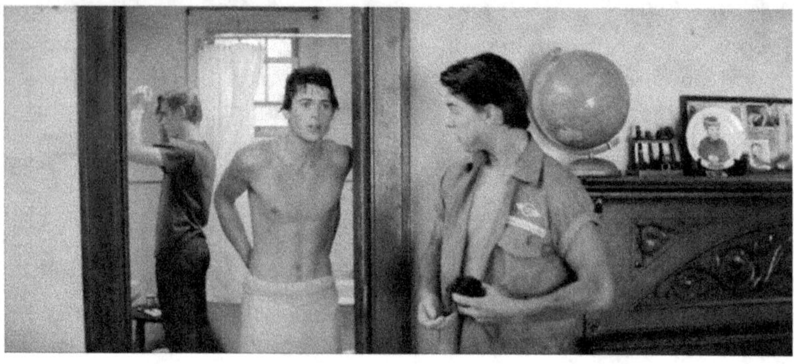

Figures 4.5 and 4.6 Shot composition that caters to a heterosexual female gaze, and a gay male one, too

Dillon provides the only moments of pleasure for adults' (73). Richard Corliss describes how Coppola's portrayal of the camaraderie among the Greasers is 'familial, embracing, unself-consciously homoerotic' (1983: 78), and while he does not go so far as to condemn the film for this portrayal, he certainly does not celebrate it, either. Nor does Andrew Sarris in the *Village Voice*, whose judgment can only be described as contemptuous:

> Much of the dialogue is so yearningly 'sensitive' that many of the lines sounded like song-cues, and many of the images are so blatantly homoerotic, what with muscular 'greasers' carrying siblings and other friends tenderly in their arms, that I was tempted to look in the final credits for Kenneth Anger's name

as a consultant on *Scorpio Rising* rituals – which is all right, if that's what today's kids think is appropriate for the expression of their innermost, acne-scarred vulnerability.

(1983)[10]

In a later, more generous analysis of *The Outsiders*, Denis Wood observes how the film's composition and lighting 'insists on the intrinsic beauty and value of these teenage boys' and how Coppola's camera 'insist[s] on the fleshly reality of the boys it caresses' (1994: 105, 111). For whom are these caresses, though? Adair, an openly gay critic, appreciates how the film 'verges on the homo-erotic' (1983), but among critics he is alone in this appreciation. Most of the reviews, written almost exclusively by heterosexual men, disparage the film for its display of male affection, its mawkishness, and the seriousness with which it treats its young characters and their lives. They conflate the heterosexual female gaze with a potentially homoerotic one, primarily because the male critics reviewing the film are not used to having their gaze disrupted. Their responses reveal at once how they recognize they are not the intended audience for *The Outsiders* and how much they revile this audience. But of course, the film is *not* for them, not for the gaze of the traditional male critic who, per Mulvey's argument, is accustomed to being the privileged viewer and thus seeing himself as the subject and women as the objects of desire on the screen (1999: 838). As Coppola himself noted, the film is for young people – especially young girls. And as Ilana Nash observes, '[a]rt forms and cultural products identified "for women" have always been less respected by our society than those identified as "for men"' (2003: 147).

Conclusion

The fundamentally opposing responses of the critics versus the teen magazines is perfectly captured in the final feature article on *The Outsiders* in *16*. The August 1983 cover announces, '*Outsiders* Review! What You Thought! What The Stars Felt! What The Critics Said!' This is *16*'s most interesting article on the movie for several reasons, not the least of which is because it includes quotes from nine different reviews. Five of them are ones I discussed earlier in this chapter – including those by Corliss and Canby. It also features 'reviews' from readers, and of the fifteen printed, three are negative. In short, *16* does not try to hide the disparity between what they call 'critical opinions' and fan reactions. In the end, though, the magazine ensures that its readers understand the most important characteristic of the film: that it was made *for them.* The article concludes by announcing that *The Outsiders* is

> A BOX OFFICE SMASH! Clearly, the critics are entitled to their opinions – just as you are entitled to yours – and perhaps, after all, it's what *you* say and feel that really counts. For in spite of the collective mixed reviews, the *Outsiders* has made oodles of money – over $20 million as *16* goes to press. And *that's* an important statistic […] What it really means is that *you* have the power to make a film into a hit – and that's something producers and movie companies do not take lightly. Perhaps, what we can expect from all this is more movies about subjects close to your heart […].
> ('*Outsiders* Review! What You Thought! What The Stars Felt! What The Critics Said!' 1983: 9, italics in original)

Validating both their readers' opinions and the heartfelt content of the movie, *16* reminds readers that 'even though adults (and most of the critics are over 35) may find fault with it, *Outsiders* is about teens, written (originally) by a teen and finally, *for* teens.' (*Outsiders* Review! What You Thought! What The Stars Felt! What The Critics Said!' 1983: 6, italics in original). In the end, the critical assessments of *The Outsiders* discussed in this chapter reveal the depths of contempt for youth interests, for adolescent female pursuits, and for representations of tenderness among adolescent males. Dismissing *The Outsiders* as trivial, the critics underestimated the impact of the film would have in the ensuing years. As I discuss in the next chapter, a robust fan culture around the movie has emerged in the past few decades, serving as a solid reminder that *The Outsiders* has remained in the hearts of viewers both past and present.

Notes

1 As of 2017, the novel has sold over 15 million copies (Krischer 2017).
2 One potential comparison is *Stand By Me* (Reiner, 1986), but the boys in this film were considerably younger than those in *The Outsiders*, and as such, they were not featured in teen magazines as prominently as Coppola's stars.
3 A small handful of critics reviewed the film positively. In 'Without Fanfare, Coppola Triumphs with *Outsiders*' Rick Lyman described the film as a 'welcome return to form' for Coppola (1983: 3D); in 'Rebels with Causes,' Joseph Gelmis offered a mild critique of the film but ultimately calls it a 'good and honorable movie' (1983: 151). Finally, Gene Siskel, a well-established and respected critic by the early 1980s, appreciated how '[t]he

teenagers in *The Outsiders* are truly noble, and on that basis I can't think of a recent movie quite like it' (1983: 3).

4 A few years after the release of *The Outsiders*, Coppola expressed his frustration over the criticism of the film:

> Many directors make movies in the same style as *The Outsiders*. The actors are good; the story was the story and that's it. Yet when I do a film like that, people now expect it to have some loaded trap door. People expect me to be nutty, weird, or at least a little unusual or strange.
>
> (quoted in Schumacher 1999: 334)

5 The decline of the teen magazine began in the early 1990s, in part due to a combination of the fragmentation of radio and the proliferation of musical genres, as well as the 'acceleration of adolescence and the shrinking number of teen idols' (Kolbert 1994: 48).

6 The only other actor in the film who was as well-known as Dillon at the time is Diane Lane. Interestingly, there is little written about her across the year-long features on the film. Only two of the twelve issues contain an article on or reference to her. The first describes how she was a target of the boys' hotel-room pranks: 'they made female cast member Diane Lane (she plays Cherry) feel right at home: they coated *her* toilet seat with honey!' ('The Making of *The Outsiders* Part 2' 1982: 11, italics in original). The second, a small profile of her along with a picture, repeats the story about the hotel hijinks but notes that she 'took it all in stride [...] and became "one of the guys" joining in pizza parties and impromptu jam sessions' ('The Making of *The* Outsiders Part 3' 1982: 31). A fascinating commentary from her, however, appears in a *Rolling Stone* article on Matt Dillon, which describes how Lane 'bears him [Dillon] a bit of a grudge. During *The Outsiders*, "We had kind of a close encounter," she confides, "but then the north wind blew." She rolls her eyes. "It was just like I wasn't there"' (Wallis 1982: 87).

7 The magazine also draws parallels between Dillon and James Dean: 'Though others liken him to the late James Dean – and he *is* flattered by the comparison – Matt wishes it would stop. "I hate this image stuff," he's said' ('Matt Dillon Countdown Part One' 1983: 24, italics in original).

8 One of the most impressive aspects of these articles is the way they encourage fans to read the book before seeing the movie. One article proclaims that if you haven't read it, 'do *not* pass "go," do not collect $200 – *run* to your local bookstore or library and pick up a copy fast!' ('The Making of *The Outsiders* Part 3' 1982: 30, italics in original). Another states that '[o]nce you've read the book, you don't quickly forget it' ('*The Outsiders* is Coming!' 1982: 17).

9 Another part of the insider status offered by *16* is its constant reminders – and updates – about the release date of *The Outsiders*. In the November 1982 issue, it tells readers to "mark your calendar for October 8" ('The Making of *The Outsiders* Part 4' 1982: 15). In the December 1982 issue, however, the story 'The Making of *The Outsiders* Part 5' is accompanied by a 'FLASH' announcement: 'As we go to press, we've just learned that Warner Brothers Films has decided to delay the premiere of *The Outsiders* until December 10 – you'll just have to wait a bit longer before you can see it. So sit back and enjoy *16*'s fantastic coverage now – it'll hold ya' till

December (when you'll have all that Christmas vacation time to see it over and over!)' ('The Making of *The Outsiders* Part 5' 1982: 15). The January 1983 issue concludes its lengthy profiles of Dillon, Macchio, and Howell with yet another announcement about the film:

> There's a saying that goes, "all good things are worth waiting for" and it looks as though you're going to have to apply that to *Outsiders* [...] The movie should have opened last month, but as you know, it didn't. The new premiere date has been set for February – but that may change as well. Anyway, *16* has taken you along every step of the way as *Outsiders* developed – and we're not about to stop now.
>
> ('The Making of *The Outsiders* Part 6' 1983: 7)

10 *Scorpio Rising* is a 1963 short film by Kenneth Anger that explores the subculture of gay male bikers.

5 'Stay gold, Ponyboy'
Nostalgia, Fandom, and *The Outsiders*

In June 2021, I booked a flight from my home in Spokane, Washington to Tulsa, Oklahoma. I was going there to visit what has quickly become the mecca of all things *Outsiders*-related: The Outsiders House Museum (see Figure 5.1). Founded by rapper Danny Boy O'Connor (former member of the hip hop band House of Pain), the Museum contains a breathtaking volume of memorabilia from the film: Coppola's director's chair, Ponyboy's sweatshirt, Johnny's jean jacket and switchblade, Dally's leather coat, and Cherry's baby blue sweater and plaid skirt; colorful, dramatic movie posters from Italy, Japan, and Taiwan; storyboards of Dally's death scene; dozens upon dozens of candid photographs taken during the filming; and countless other images and props. It also boasts a remarkable collection of the many versions of Hinton's novel, a visual reminder of the myriad ways the book has been imagined by cover designers and living proof of the fact that it has been translated into over 30 languages (Krischer 2017). All of this memorabilia resides at 731 North St. Louis Avenue, in the very same house used during the filming of *The Outsiders*: the Curtis brothers' home, which functions as the home for most of the other Greasers as well.[1] Painstakingly renovated and carefully appointed with furniture and décor as close to those featured in the film, The Outsiders House Museum welcomes a steady stream of visitors four days a week. Fans of all ages, races, sexes, and socioeconomic classes come from all over the U.S., walking through the doors of the house to revisit the magic of the story and to participate in a collective desire to stay gold. Only three years into existence, the Museum has cemented the cult status of *The Outsiders*.

Truth be told, my trip to the House was as much for pleasure as for business. When I found out about its existence, I knew a visit would be necessary for this project. But the idea of it also thrilled me as a fan, and my private tour of the Museum allowed me to examine every object, every detail of the space. As is the case for many visitors, I held

DOI: 10.4324/9781003228783-6

Figure 5.1 The Outsiders House Museum, located at 731 N. St. Louis Avenue in Tulsa, Oklahoma; the intersection on which the house sits has been renamed as The Outsiders Way and the Curtis Brothers Lane (image courtesy of the author)

a replica of the towel – signed by Rob Lowe! – that Sodapop wrapped around his wet torso after showering. I watched television like Two-Bit, on the living room floor with a beer in one hand and a prop piece of chocolate cake in the other. Most memorably, I sat at the desk where Ponyboy wrote his English paper; there, in the notebook, the famous opening line of the novel is scrawled in the handwriting of an adult C. Thomas Howell. I am not embarrassed to admit that the entire experience moved me to tears. But why? I had no real connection to this house and the objects in it. I had only a profound childhood connection to the story, the actors, and the memory of seeing them play it out in the very spaces where I stood.

In her landmark study *The Future of Nostalgia*, Svetlana Boym explains how nostalgia 'is a longing for home that no longer exists or has never existed' (2001: xiii). It is also 'a yearning for a different time – the time of our childhood, the slower rhythm of our dreams' (xv). Certainly some of these emotions – longing and yearning – were at work in my visit to the Museum. But the Museum, and more broadly all things *Outsiders*-related, elicit more than these emotions. They connote not only a remembrance of the past but also a desire for community and belonging in the present. In this chapter, I explore the cult status of *The Outsiders* as exemplified in the Museum and the enduring power of the phrase 'Stay gold.' I argue that The Outsiders House Museum and the larger industry around *The Outsiders* – book and film alike – participate in a very particular kind of nostalgia, one linked inherently to fan culture. Like nostalgia, fandom is 'always partly private and partly social' (Hills 2013: viii); as such, the two experiences parallel and inform each other. The 'network' of *Outsiders* fans is small but enthusiastic and loyal, and the family they create – with the House as the primary gathering site and the source of nostalgia – is one of deep emotional connection.

Nostalgia: Concept and Experience

As a concept and an experience, nostalgia has been studied by historians, sociologists, and cultural theorists, among others. Among them, it is widely agreed that the term was first identified and named over three hundred years ago in 1688, when Swiss physician Johannes Hofer published his dissertation on the topic. Hofer used the term to describe the complaints of 'displaced soldiers, domestic workers and students who developed symptoms in response to their profound homesickness' (Pallister 2019: 2). '[U]sing the Greek roots *nostos*, which means returning to a native area, and *algos*, a term for pain or grief,' Hofer categorized nostalgia as a medical condition, an illness or disease (Winter 2022). The negative connotations associated with nostalgia continued well into the twentieth century in the Western world; in his 1966 essay 'The Idea of Nostalgia,' Swiss literary critic Jean Starobinski observed how the term had 'taken on a pejorative connotation [...] impl[ying] the useless yearning for a world or for a way of life from which one has been irrevocably severed' (1966: 125). Often associated with immaturity, sentimentality, and conservatism, the concept was derided by critics for decades, particularly in the 1970s and 1980s. In his well-known essay 'The Politics of Nostalgia,' cultural critic Christopher Lasch summarizes this negative view of nostalgia: '[t]o cling to the past is bad enough, but the victim of nostalgia clings to an idealized past, one that exists only in his [sic] head' (1984: 65).

More recently, however, nostalgia has undergone a thoughtful reappraisal. The desire both to reevaluate and to complicate nostalgia is reflected in the work of critics such as cultural theorist Boym, sociologist Janelle L. Wilson, and historian Tobias Becker. In his essay 'The Meanings of Nostalgia: Genealogy and Critique,' for example, Becker examines how historians have been dismissive of nostalgia, seeing it as a one-dimensional and inherently problematic experience rather than choosing to 'closely investigate the ways in which people engage with and make sense of the past and to find out about their motivations' (2018: 250). Becker calls on scholars to 'take nostalgia seriously instead of parroting well-rehearsed arguments of cultural decline' (ibid.). Wilson is among those who take nostalgia seriously, understanding it not as 'a mere passive longing for the past, but a potentially dynamic vehicle for (re)envisioning and (re)creating various pasts and futures' (2015: 490).[2] She counts herself among the 'many contemporary scholars [who] deem nostalgia a positive experience that provides individuals with the opportunity to reflect upon their past and to incorporate change into the more familiar background of previous experiences' (481).

There are many different ways to look at nostalgia, then; different methods for conceptualizing it. Most useful for thinking about *The Outsiders*, Wilson theorizes nostalgia as a yearning for both a time and a place. 'Nostalgic experiences are anchored in space,' she says, and 'as we recollect or remember, the experience of nostalgia is embodied. That is to say, we recall both a place and a time and we also recall our lived experience associated with the memory' (2015: 479). I am interested in using Wilson's framework of nostalgia for analyzing the phenomenon of *The Outsiders*, not only because The Outsiders House Museum is a material manifestation of the ways in which nostalgia is 'anchored in space,' but also because the film's relationship and legacy vis-à-vis nostalgia is at once complicated and distinct from that of other 1980s teen films. It is to this latter point that I turn in the next section.

Nostalgia for the '80s: Teen Films and Memory

As examined in Chapter 2, the genre of teen films experienced a remarkable renaissance in the 1980s. As a result, many of the '80s movies about which contemporary viewers, young and old alike, feel nostalgic are adolescent films. From stories of sexually active, pot-smoking teens like *Fast Times at Ridgemont High* to heartfelt, iconic movies of the underdog making a name for himself like *The Karate Kid* (Avildsen, 1984) to silly adventure films featuring a group of misfits like *The Goonies* (Donner, 1985), numerous '80s teen films have robust, enthusiastic followings, and the current discourse about them appreciates them for the way in which they capture the feel and zeitgeist of the 1980s. Perhaps none do so more than the quintessential teen films of the 1980s, the John Hughes triad of *Sixteen Candles, The Breakfast Club*, and *Pretty in Pink*. In her volume on *The Breakfast Club* for this series, Elissa H. Nelson considers Hughes' film within the larger context of 1980s teen films and concludes that it is 'an exemplary teen film […] a product of its specific era' (2019: 100). Situated among other adolescent films of the era and our nostalgic relationship to them, *The Outsiders* is yet again an outlier. Set in the mid-1960s but not deeply invested – narratively, politically, or aesthetically – in that era, *The Outsiders* does not aim to turn back time as did earlier films such as *Grease* or later ones such as *Dirty Dancing*. The kind of nostalgia that *The Outsiders* engenders as opposed to these films, or contemporaneous ones like *Fast Times at Ridgemont High* or *Sixteen Candles*, stems from two aspects of the movie. The first is its story: told by a 14-year-old boy, the narrative structure invites a return to childhood, as I further discuss later. The second is the casting, which retrospectively invites nostalgia. In her volume on *Grease* for this series, Barbara Jane Brickman contends that despite being set in the 1950s, the film's 'teenager is a 1970s teenager' (2018: 11).[3] Similarly, despite being set in the 1960s, the teenagers of *The Outsiders* are 1980s teenagers. Looking back on the film, then, we are invited to marvel at the moment right before the Brat Pack exploded on the Hollywood scene – the moment that these young men don't know is about to happen, but we now do.

Published in the June 1985 issue of *New York* magazine, David Blum's now-infamous article 'Hollywood's Brat Pack' was instrumental in naming and establishing the up-and-coming cohort of young actors in Hollywood – mostly male – who 'exude[d] a magnetic force' and, concomitantly, had a powerful grip on the industry. Noting the ubiquity of the Brat Pack, their image on screens everywhere, Blum asserts that

> […] it would be a major achievement for the average American moviegoer not to have seen at least one of their ensemble movies over the past four years. The first Brat Pack movie was *Taps*, the story of kids taking over a military school, a sleeper that took in $20.5 million. Then came *The Outsiders*, adapted from the S. E. Hinton novel and directed by Francis Ford Coppola; *Rumble Fish*, another Coppola-Hinton effort; *The Breakfast Club*; and now, on June 28, the release of the latest matchup of the Brats, *St. Elmo's Fire*.
>
> (1985)

Blum describes how the actors – Emilio Estevez, Rob Lowe, Judd Nelson, and an ancillary group including Matt Dillon and Sean Penn – 'make major movies with big directors and get fat contracts and limousines. They have top agents and protective P.R. people. They have legions of fans who write them letters, buy them drinks, follow them home. And, most important, they sell movie tickets' (1985). At once identifying the young actors as a powerful force in Hollywood, suggesting that few of them have real talent, and maligning them for their spoiled, juvenile behavior, Blum's article 'made the kind of immediate zeitgeist splash that was rare in the pre-Internet era' (Argetsinger 2015); it created a label that stuck immediately and remains today. *The Outsiders* is seen – by Blum then and by fans now – as one of the first entries in the Brat Pack oeuvre. Indeed, even though only two of the seven actors in *The Outsiders* were members of the elite group of the Pack, a recent article in *The Independent* ranks the movie as number one on a list of the '10 Best Brat Pack films' (Loughrey 2020), and a contemporary review of the film's restored cut identifies it as 'Coppola's Brat Pack Melodrama' (Bradshaw 2021).[4]

Part of the nostalgia associated with *The Outsiders* stems from the knowledge we have now of what these actors' futures will look like; we know what is to come for them. Indeed, Timothy Shary marvels over the fact that Coppola 'cast the film with almost *every single young male star* of the next decade [...] I don't think anyone can name another film in Hollywood history that launched (or propelled) the careers of so many young stars – and not just the guys, but also Diane Lane and Sofia Coppola' (2022, italics in original). Amy Amatangelo concurs, stating that '[w]atching *The Outsiders* now is an evocative experience' and that the film 'is now legendary because of its cast' (2021). In relation to the cast, the nostalgia it engenders, then, is twofold: it is both knowing look back to the past, and for those of us who are old enough to have been around when the film came out, a remembrance of the energy and excitement around these young stars who would soon explode on the scene. And then, the '80s teen film would take a new direction with John Hughes.

But the nostalgia associated with *The Outsiders* is more than just a wistful recollection of the birth of the Brat Pack. It is also tied to the narrative of the movie and its source: Ponyboy as narrator and Hinton as author. Few teen films of the 1980s feature a child on the cusp of teenage life as their narrator, which means few of them invite viewer identification in quite the same way as does *The Outsiders*.[5] Further, few teen films of the 1980s have a built-in audience because of the book that preceded it. In the 40 years since the film's release, the book continues to enjoy a steady and loyal readership in the U.S. primarily but worldwide as well, as evidenced by the aforementioned number of translations. The movie thus attracts legions of new fans through the book, and fans young and old alike flock to the Museum to engage more deeply in the world that is *The Outsiders*. Barbara Jane Brickman observes how Hollywood movies of the late 1970s-early 1980s relied upon a 'transmedia synergy' to sell tickets (2018: 28) – a strategy that involved marketing the film across various media, including advertising, soundtracks, and music videos. Nelson defines synergy as 'the idea that products related to one intellectual property, if sold across different media and ancillary markets, could exponentially increase sale and recognition of said property' (2019: 20). While *The Outsiders* was nowhere near a blockbuster film in the vein of *Grease* or *The Breakfast Club*, it benefited from the small scale synergy of the longevity of the book and its relationship to the film. Indeed, this synergy has helped the movie maintain currency throughout the years, as it is regularly taught alongside the novel in the U.S., thus contributing to its nostalgic roots. And many of those middle and high school readers, both past and present, take a trip to The Outsiders House Museum as the culmination of their reading experience.

'The Fandom is Real': The Outsiders House Museum as Home

The driving force behind the founding and success of The Outsiders House Museum is Danny Boy O'Connor. His path to what he calls 'the greatest thing that's ever happened to me' was circuitous (2021). A former rapper best known for his membership in the hip-hop group House of Pain (their biggest hit, 'Jump Around,' is routinely played at sporting events), O'Connor came to his calling by accident. Visiting Tulsa on a tour in 2009, he asked a cab driver if any of the locations from the filming of *The Outsiders* were available to view. The cab driver took him all over town – to the Admiral Twin Drive-In, to North Tulsa, and to Crutchfield Park, where several scenes were shot, and finally to the House at 731 North St. Louis Drive. 'I remember being in front of the house and just being in awe' (quoted in Ethington 2021). Mesmerized, O'Connor surveyed the house and wondered: 'Why isn't anybody seeing what I'm seeing? A golden opportunity, pun intended' (2021). His mind was flooded with questions: Why was it in such disrepair? Didn't anyone know or care about its history? And was it for sale?

Turns out, several years later it was, for $50,000 – a price tag O'Connor could not afford at the time. But he kept his eye on it, checking its sale status every year, and finally in 2016 he bought it for $14,000. Over the course of three years and with the help of dozens upon dozens of people, in particular his right-hand man in the business, Donnie Rich, O'Connor renovated the house – which was in such a serious state of disrepair that he thought, 'I have bitten off so much more than I can chew' (quoted in Ethington 2021). They opened the Museum in August 2019. 'My original plan was not a museum,' O'Connor said, but his vision changed: fueled by his childhood connection to the film and his longtime interest in movie memorabilia, the House became one (2021). One of O'Connor's friends and colleagues, George Carroll (also known as Boston rapper Slaine), explains that 'Danny has a very creative mind and also a very nostalgic one' (quoted in Ethington 2021), and he uses his love of nostalgia to build an empire of *Outsiders* fandom. Since its opening, The Outsiders House Museum has become a popular tourist destination in Tulsa (as of this writing, it boasts 4.7/5 stars with over 500 reviews on Google), a mecca for fans both within the state and around the country. On any given weekend, travelers from Oklahoma and Texas will pay a visit, as will tourists from as far away as California and Georgia. While most visitors hail from the U.S., the Museum has attracted fans from Canada, the U.K., Japan, and Australia as well. Michael Fellwock, one of the lead tour guides, estimates that 150 people a day go through the Museum. 'It's a destination,' Fellwock says, attracting people from all walks of life – 'rich, poor, Greaser, Soc,' cutting across categories of age, gender, race, and sexual orientation – and the connective thread is the visitors' love of the book, the movie, or both (2021).

I have visited the Museum several times now, including for the weekend celebration of the release of the 4K 40th Anniversary Edition of *The Outsiders: The Complete Novel.* What is most striking about the fandom related to The Outsiders House Museum is the sense of family and belonging that it engenders in both its visitors and its Facebook and Twitter followers. O'Connor observes that one of the aspects of the Museum that contributes to its success and near-icon status is its 'multigenerational appeal' (quoted in Ethington 2021), and this is precisely what I observed in the four days I spent there. The youngest visitor was around age four, the oldest around 70. A couple in their 50s had driven eight hours from Nebraska just to visit the Museum. A grandmother brought her grandkids to the House; they had recently read the book and watched the film in class. A dad with five kids, ages four through 12, walked through the doors; the children immediately scattered, running excitedly to different rooms in the house. A group of men in their 20s, all players on a regional baseball team, stopped in to visit between games. That evening, before the film viewing on the lawn on the House, I met a family of four who had flown in from Georgia; the oldest daughter was celebrating her 16th birthday, and a visit to the Curtis Brothers' House was her requested gift. During the movie, I sat next to a couple in their 60s from Tulsa; they told me how happy they were with how Danny had built up the house, the neighborhood, and the town. The groups were all ages and all races and ethnicities: Native, white, Hispanic, African-American. Throughout the day, two of the main tour guides, Fellwock and Dana Wirth Ludwig, welcomed visitors into the house as if it were their own. They shared stories about the making of the film, with Fellwock joking about being 'Rob Lowe's body double' and Ludwig dishing on her close encounter with Matt Dillon during the filming of *The Outsiders* (when she was a teenager, she tracked him down at the Excelsior Hotel and partied with him, Lowe, and Cruise). Theirs was a nostalgia that was not exclusive or cliquish but rather inclusive and inviting – an 'affective nostalgia' defined 'not merely [by] a longing for a *past* community' (Wilson 2015: 482, italics in original) but rather one with 'the potential to create positive affect and solidarity for community in the present' (Holyfield et al. 2013: 459). That solidarity is apparent from the minute you walk up to the House and are greeted by the tour guides to the moment you leave and are invited to join the 'for fans only' Facebook group, the Friends of 731 N. St. Louis Avenue.

Because of the impact and ongoing significance of the book, the fandom of *The Outsiders* also differs from that of most other '80s teen movies. James Mockoski, film archivist and restoration supervisor for American Zoetrope, contends that the novel and movie are a 'good pairing [...] you can't have one without the other' (2021). There are, of course, fans of the film who have not read the book or were not familiar with Hinton's novel before viewing the movie, and their love of *The Outsiders* is not diminished as a result. But Mockoski's assertion is nonetheless borne out in the Museum. Indeed, O'Connor himself recognizes the dual purposes that the House serves: 'I thought I was building a movie museum; what I found out is that I was building a literary museum' (2021). He perhaps undersells the visitors' emotional connection to the House as the site of the film, but he also rightly acknowledges that there would be no House *without* the book. And no other iconic teen movie continues to draw younger generations to it the way *The Outsiders* does. Young fans of the film often discover its existence through the book; in Tulsa, for example, *The Outsiders* is required reading in the public middle-school curriculum, and many of these students watch the movie and visit the Museum as the culmination of their reading experience. In this way, '*The Outsiders* is like a rite of passage,' says O'Connor (quoted in Ethington 2021).

Whether the rite of passage happens when reading Hinton's book, seeing Coppola's film, or both, the initiation into *The Outsiders* often involves a deep sense of emotional connection to the story and/or an identification with one or more of the characters. Within the fan culture of *The Outsiders*, those experiences are often most readily and succinctly expressed in the story's signature line: 'Stay gold.' This is philosophy of life that *Outsiders* fans share with each other through communications on Facebook and Twitter (#staygold) and on electronic messages (e.g., those associated with the House will often use 'Stay gold' to sign off on email). 'Staying gold' and its partner phrase – 'Nothing gold can stay' – signify the importance of innocence, of viewing the world not through skeptical, ironic eyes but through hopeful, generous ones. Indeed, in an interview, S.E. Hinton explained what she meant by the phrase: 'Gold is openness to other people, an ability to empathize with other human beings. I think you're more likely to have that when you're young. You compromise as you get older' (Campbell 1985: 62). In our current historical moment, an era that privileges an attitude of acrimony and mistrust, the 'compromise' to which Hinton refers often requires either a detachment from authentic feeling or a skepticism toward it – and toward nostalgia as well. Cultural critic Linda Hutcheon asserts that our postmodern era encourages 'the ironizing of nostalgia' (2000: 207). Notably, there is not a shred of irony vis-à-vis *The Outsiders* and particularly in and around the Museum.[6] Rather, there is a feeling of admiration and adoration for these stories and characters, untarnished by adult cynicism. 'Stay gold' functions, then, as a verbal shortcut. It expresses a sense of belonging to and membership in the fan community, and, as an imperative sentence, it stresses the importance of resisting the pessimism and judgment that often characterize adult life.

Niklas Salmose asserts that nostalgia is at once 'an emotional experience and an aesthetic modality' (2019: 1). If 'Stay gold' exemplifies the emotional experience of *The Outsiders*, then the image of the Greaser – and the other signature line from the film, 'Do it for Johnny' – personifies its aesthetic experience. Passionately pronounced by Dally right before the rumble between the Greasers and the Socs, 'Do it for Johnny' expresses the Greaser belief in loyalty and love against all odds. Like 'Stay gold,' this phrase is of course emotional as well, but its primary expression occurs through the various experiences offered by the Museum. Visitors are invited to re-enact scenes of the film – all of which are Greaser-only scenes, since it is the Curtis's home – but also to purchase Greaser-themed items in the gift shop. Indeed, the only non-Greaser item offered for sale is a yellow shirt that says 'Socs' on the back, and it is a replica of one worn by the Soc actors during the making of the film in 1982. If '[n]ostalgia connotes emotion, thought, and in some sense, behavior' (Wilson 1999: 299), then the behavior encouraged by The Outsiders House Museum specifically and the larger fan base generally is one aligned with a Greaser ethos. Fans express their allegiance to that ethos in various ways. They wear shirts that say 'Stay gold, Ponyboy' or 'The Outsiders House Museum' on them. They have their picture taken while pretending to push-start Two-Bit's car. They clothe themselves to look just like the characters. The most impressive of this latter group of fans are the Twin Greasers, aka the Admiral Twins, two adolescent girls from Nebraska who dressed up as the different characters from *The Outsiders* and recreated various scenes from the film on location. Fans on the Facebook page loved their homage. In the fan world of *The Outsiders*, nostalgia for the book and film 'serves as a repository of social connectedness' (Routledge et al. 2012: 453). As Hayley Krischer proclaims, 'Once you're a fan of "The Outsiders," you're always a fan of "The Outsiders"' (2017).

In the course of the year during which I researched and wrote this book, The Outsiders House Museum welcomed some high-profile visitors. In early July 2021, Leonardo DiCaprio, who was nearby on location for a film, stopped by to visit. (He was wearing a mask and thus made his way through the Museum undetected.) A week later, the members of the punk rock band Green Day surprised the staff with a visit; the lead singer, Billie Joe Armstrong, sat at Ponyboy's desk just like any other fan and posed for an Instagram picture. Then in March 2022, Dally himself, Matt Dillon, returned to the House for the first time in almost 40 years; he was accompanied by S.E. Hinton. These occasions increased the Museum's visibility and cultural cache, highlighting its appeal across generations – and underscoring how the fan base has grown substantially since the early 1980s. Teen girls were the primary devotees of the film in the early 1980s, and teen girls today still walk through the doors of the Museum in large numbers. But so, too, to Gen-Xers who saw the movie 40 years ago (Fellwock 2021). This older crowd, however, consists not only of women who were once the squealing girls in 1983 but also of adult men like O'Connor who, based on his own childhood experiences, strongly identified with the characters. 'I could relate to the story so much,' he said (quoted in Ethington 2021); to him, the characters 'seemed very authentic' (O'Connor 2021). 'I took the style with me [...] it was that Dallas Winston swagger that I was trying to be like' (ibid.). That swagger, part of the Greasers' aesthetic, draws an adult male heterosexual fan base. And, as I will discuss in the Concluding chapter, it also draws a notable queer following as well. If nostalgia is 'the self-focused emotional process through which people recollect experiences that imbue their lives with meaning' (Routledge et al. 2012: 459), then The Outsiders House Museum provides fans with the literal and figurative space in which to experience that process. Nostalgia is a longing for 'a home that is both physical and spiritual' (Boym 2001: 8). For fans of *The Outsiders*, the Museum is that home.

Conclusion

Critiques of nostalgia are often grounded in the belief that looking back means refusing to live in the present in an authentic way. In his essay 'Nostalgia Critique,' Stuart Tannock explains how scholars who view nostalgia as a negative experience assume that the term almost exclusively 'invokes a positively evaluated past world in response to a deficient present world' (1995: 454). This tendency to look back at the past as ideal, according to some critics, is 'pathological, regressive, and delusional' (455). Mark Duffett identifies a parallel critique of fandom: that fans 'resemble ideal brand consumers' and as such are dupes whose 'fandom is primarily *about* consumption' (2013: 21, italics in original), not about a genuine connection to the media source. While Tannock and Duffett do not deny that nostalgia and fandom are complex concepts, especially with regard to politics and consumerism respectively, they reject the broad sweep of these claims. Rather, Tannock proposes that nostalgia 'responds to a diversity of personal needs and political desires' (1995: 454), including the desire for community. Duffett points out that fans are 'more than consumers because they have especially strong emotional attachments to their objects and they use them to create relationships with both their heroes and with each other' (2013: 21).

Enshrined in The Outsiders House Museum, the story of *The Outsiders* – the book, the making of the film, and the legacy of both – fills a variety of personal needs and enables unexpected and fulfilling emotional attachments. For Michael, an extroverted, affable Gen-Xer, the House is a place where he can be fully himself – where he can welcome people and invite them into the *Outsiders* community.

For Claire, a young woman in her 20s who lost both her parents when she was 15, the House is a reminder of one of her favorite memories of her dad and a place to heal the brokenness that comes with loss. For Eric, who runs an auto restoration and detailing business, being part of what he calls 'The Outsiders Empire' allows him to feel like a kid again. Meeting them and so many other fans was a lesson for me how the motto 'Stay gold' has come to mean many things to many different people, all of them inextricably linked to the feeling of kinship revealed in the film. Historian David Loewenthal remarks that often '[n]ostalgia is blamed for alienating people from the present' (1985: 13). But the fans of *The Outsiders* who visit the Museum are living very much in the moment, forging bonds with other devotees of the book and movie. Danny Boy O'Connor mused, 'I can't tell you many forty year old movies that still stay in the public eye like this one does' (O'Connor 2021). Nor can I. Indeed, only a handful of youth cinema from the 1980s – *Sixteen Candles, The Breakfast Club, Ferris Bueller's Day Off*, and *Dirty Dancing* – have remained in pop culture consciousness in the same way as *The Outsiders*. In the final chapter of this book, I survey the ways in which *The Outsiders* and its portrait of adolescent tenderness and staying gold has endured.

Notes

1 In 'Tales of Sound and Fury: Observations on the Family Melodrama,' Thomas Elsaesser notes how the setting of the family melodrama is the home itself (1987: 61). The significance of the Curtis house vis-à-vis the film narrative thus reinforces the melodramatic underpinnings of *The Outsiders*; the image of it functions as the one lone establishing shot that is repeatedly identifiable. Though the house is on screen for only approximately seventeen minutes in *The Complete Novel*, it has become the iconic gathering site for fans.

2 Wilson acknowledges her indebtedness to sociologist Fred Davis, whose landmark study *Yearning for Yesterday: A Sociology of Nostalgia* (1979) established nostalgia as an area worthy of academic study. She observes how '[w]ith both second-order and third-order types of nostalgia, as described by Davis, there is an active engagement with the past rather than the mere passive "longing" that characterizes first-order nostalgia' (Wilson 2015: 480).

3 While *The Outsiders* perhaps invites nostalgia via certain aspects of its aesthetics – the costumes, setting, and dialogue are all era-appropriate – I would argue that the purpose of these aesthetics is *not* a yearning to return to this era. In contrast to the poodle skirts in *Grease* or the very specific setting of Kellerman's country club in *Dirty Dancing*, the costumes, setting, and dialogue are meant to bring authenticity to the story but are not its central affective focal point. Put another way, *The Outsiders* lacks the period specificity

of other nostalgic films, and in this way it differs from those movies that clearly invite a nostalgic response (a point I discuss briefly in Chapter 3).

4 In his article 'Which 1980s Teen Stars Were Members Of The Brat Pack?' Michael Kennedy points out how '[a]nother common inclusion in some Brat Pack rosters is the cast of Francis Ford Coppola's *The Outsiders* [...] While they were all rising young stars of the 1980s, and founding members Estevez and Lowe did appear in *The Outsiders*, only Swayze worked with any core Brat Pack members afterward' (2021).

5 Worth noting is that Rob Reiner's 1986 film *Stand By Me* employs a similar narrative framework as *The Outsiders*, i.e., a male writer reflecting on past friendships. The difference, however, is that *Stand By Me*'s narrator is now an adult looking back on his youth, whereas Ponyboy is still an adolescent, still awaiting his future.

6 Interestingly (and perhaps ironically), film critic Armand White identifies the lack of irony as the reason for the 'failure' of *The Outsiders*. Identifying it and *Rumble Fish* as Coppola's 'Boy Movies,' White makes the following claim: 'At once stirring and embarrassing, the Boy Movies failed not because of stylistic excess but from total lack of irony' (1985: 10).

Conclusion

The Legacy of *The Outsiders*

At the time of its release, *The Outsiders* was embraced by a teen audience, and its profits were strong enough that it was considered a moderate success at the box office. They were not, however, significant enough that the film would be distinguished as a teen blockbuster like some of its contemporaries, including *Risky Business*, *Footloose*, or *Ferris Bueller's Day Off*. Within a few years, Coppola's film had been eclipsed by the more popular and more immediately influential adolescent films of John Hughes, specifically the trifecta of *Sixteen Candles, The Breakfast Club,* and *Ferris Bueller's Day Off*. Unlike *The Outsiders*, these movies were set in the contemporary moment and thus reflected more explicitly the specific social anxieties of 1980s teens. By the end of the decade, youth cinema had also taken a darker, more cynical turn with films like *River's Edge* (Hunter, 1987) and *Heathers*. In comparison, *The Outsiders* seemed outdated in its earnestness.

Nonetheless, the film remained visible on 1980s pop culture landscapes thanks to the boom in the home video market. Released on VHS in 1983 and Laserdisc in 1987, and watched by thousands of people via these media, *The Outsiders* maintained a steady fan base across the decade. As a result of the film's success across these media formats, by 1989 a television series based on the book and film had been developed, with Coppola himself as the executive producer. Picked up by the then-burgeoning Fox network, the hour-long drama debuted in March 1990, seven years after the premiere of the film. It fared well with the critics and attracted a strong audience for its 90-minute pilot, but the following episodes did not draw impressive numbers; by May 1990, the network had decided to cancel it (Jay 2022).[1] But its very existence underscores the influence of the book and film. Reminders of *The Outsiders*' significance as a 1980s teen film would emerge in various moments across the ensuing years: in 2005, when Coppola released *The Outsiders: The Complete Novel* on DVD;

DOI: 10.4324/9781003228783-7

on the film's 30th anniversary in 2013; on the 50th anniversary of the novel in 2017; and most recently, in 2021, when Coppola released the 4K restoration of *The Complete Novel* and the film made its way back to theaters for a short run.

I have seen *The Outsiders: The Complete Novel* four times in theaters: at the Admiral Twin Drive-In and at the Circle Cinema, both sites where the movie was filmed; on the lawn of The Outsiders House Museum; and finally, at the Garland Theater, the same place where I saw the movie on its opening night in 1983. On every one of these occasions, I was struck by the range of people in the audience. There were women my age, to be sure, likely original fangirls excited to see their childhood crushes on the screen again. There were heterosexual couples, Gen-Xers on dates. There were families with preteen children; single adult men watching the movie by themselves; teenagers in pairs chatting excitedly before the lights dimmed. When the film ended and credits rolled at the Garland Theater, the audience applauded and a young man in his 30s sitting behind me yelled with approval, 'Hell, yeah!' *The Outsiders* fan base might not be as large as those of other 1980s teen films like *The Breakfast Club*, but it is a loyal, enthusiastic one, a community of Greasers with big hearts.

While movie theaters and the Museum function as the physical site for nostalgia and fandom, the Internet functions as the virtual site of these experiences. Some scholars of fan culture identify the participation in a 'consumption-based community' as part of fandom (Duffett 2013: 31), and this is certainly borne out in the wide range of *Outsiders*-related merchandise that any die-hard fan can find on the Internet. Such merchandise is available in person and online at The Outsiders House Museum, of course, where the gift shop capitalizes on the Greaser ethos via a wide range of products, from the unembellished zip hoodies with the Museum's name and location on them, to the black t-shirts featuring a switchblade and the quote 'Let's do it for Johnny, man.' Everything at the Museum gift shop is cool; the aesthetic skews toward the masculine, emphasizing the toughness of the Greasers. Online – particularly on Etsy, self-described as 'the global marketplace for unique and creative goods' – the inventory of *Outsiders*-related products favors the whimsical, sentimental, even romantic. Etsy's aesthetic is feminine, targeting either current adolescent female fans of the book and movie, or past ones like myself. This is not entirely surprising, given that 'as of 2017, 81% of all buyers on Etsy were female' (Peters no date). Interestingly, however, 'the majority of Etsy buyers [are] between 25-40 years of age,' and '15% of them [are] younger than the age of 25' (ibid.) – which means that many of the consumers of these products are not the Gen-Xers who saw the movie in 1983, but younger fans who have only recently discovered *The Outsiders,* whether through their parents, their schools, or their interest in '80s nostalgia. And these fans have literally thousands of products from which to choose: die-cut stickers of the characters or of quotes like 'Nothing gold can stay'; pendant necklaces or earrings with the characters' images on them; 'Smells Like Ponyboy' candles; collectible shot glasses with an image of the entire cast on them; and fleece blankets featuring the movie poster. For a cheekier selection of items, fans can head over to RedBubble – a site that aims to 'give independent artists a meaningful new way to sell their creations' – and purchase a mini-skirt with Sodapop's face plastered across it or a t-shirt that reads, 'Dallas Winston? You mean my husband?' That *The Outsiders* has such a healthy online retail presence bespeaks its staying power, its affective pull to fans old and new.

While some scholars complain that 'fandom is primarily *about* but consumption,' Duffett pushes back on this notion, asserting that fans 'are *always already* consumers – as we all are – but they necessarily have more roles than that' (2013: 21, italics in original). They are also 'networkers, collectors, tourists, archivists, curators, producers and more' (ibid.). Of these roles, another prominent online role is that of producer – specifically, the creator of *Outsiders*-themed fan fiction. As of this writing, there are almost 9000 entries on *The Outsiders* available fanfiction.net and another thousand on wattpad.com. Matt Hills observes that '[f]ans interpret media texts in a variety of interesting and perhaps unexpected ways' (2002: ix), and this is certainly the case with *The Outsiders.* Some fan fiction authors imagine new scenarios with the original characters; others create entirely original characters, like Johnny's little sister named Jennie, Dally's cousin Harry, or a 'Curtis Sister.' Fan fiction is also the site where queer fandom emerges most clearly. Transforming the homosocial bonds between Ponyboy, Johnny, and Dally, and the other Greasers into homoerotic ones, a sizable portion of the fan fiction imagines romantic and sexual relationships between the young men. This reworking of *The Outsiders* is not entirely unexpected. As Michelle Ann Abate observes, Hinton's novel is 'laden with homoerotic overtones. The central male characters frequently touch, cuddle, and express their affection for each other in intimate ways' (2017: 55). More humorously, Nathan Rabin notes how the film, with its images of desirable young men and the sometimes half-dressed male adolescent bodies of Dally and Soda, is 'extraordinarily homoerotic, a macho yet totally emo tale of beautiful, jacked-up men who stare at each other with intense cryptic gazes, almost as if they can't decide whether they want to punch or kiss their adversary' (2015). As I discussed in Chapter 4, some film critics disparaged *The Outsiders* for this very reason. Rather than allow that disparagement to stand, queer fan fiction embraces the story's homoeroticism, imagining worlds that invite a multiplicity of desire and identification.[2]

Whether as an enthusiastic creator of fan or slash fiction, an amateur archivist contributing to *The Outsiders* Wiki, or an eager tourist visiting The Outsiders House Museum, fans can find a home among like-minded people who appreciate both the story and the sentiment of *The Outsiders*. Those people include British superfan Katie Sawyer, whose Twitter name and handle Pity the Back Seat is an homage to *The Outsiders*. She regularly tweets about the film, the actors, Hinton, and Coppola, sharing *Outsiders*-related photos and sources with her fellow fans. They include Hinton herself, who is exceptionally active on Twitter; she occasionally shares memories of the filmmaking process and the actors with whom she became friends. And they include the creative minds behind the forthcoming musical based on *The Outsiders*, which will debut in 2023 at the La Jolla Playhouse Theatre in San Diego.[3] In a world saturated with media both old and new, the fact that Coppola's *The Outsiders* has remained a cultural touchstone 40 years after its release is at once unexpected and extraordinary. Its longevity can be attributed to many factors: the book's continued inclusion in middle- and high-school curriculum in the U.S.; the movie's unique directorial pedigree in the 1980s teen film genre; the fact that it 'launched the careers of the biggest stars of the Brat Pack era and beyond' (Macnab 2021); and most importantly, the fan base that keeps the legacy of the film alive.

In recent years, both the film's impact and its quality have been reconsidered by scholars and critics. In *Generation Multiplex*, Timothy Shary included *The Outsiders* alongside *Fast Times at Ridgemont High, The Breakfast Club,* and *Risky Business* on a short list of films that he considers 'Most Influential to Other Youth Films' (2014: 337). Of *The Outsiders*, Shary contends that 'there's really few other teen films of that era that even come close to its resonance and quality' (2022). The BFI, too, included *The Outsiders* on a list of 'great American teen films of the 1980s' (Baughn 2018), and *The Guardian*'s film critic, Peter Bradshaw, gave the 4K version a five-star review (2021). After years of being viewed as an insignificant effort on Coppola's part and an anachronistic entry in '80s youth cinema, *The Outsiders* is finally having its day in the sun. From the film's inception, Coppola identified his audience – young people – and his intent in making *The Outsiders*: to validate the emotions and experiences of kids. As Coppola shares in his commentary on the 4K version of the film, 'I've always instinctively felt that young people are capable of profound feelings of love and friendship and loyalty' ('An Introduction … ' 2021). In a 1982 interview in *Variety*, Coppola described *The Outsiders* as 'a movie about youth, but a movie for kids of grown-up proportions. It's not a little picture. It's a heartbreaking story, with nobility' (quoted in McCarthy 1982: 172). As a result of his generous attitude toward the source material, *The Outsiders* 'doesn't condescend to kids' (Burns 2018); it takes them and their feelings seriously. Despite its initially unforgiving reviews, 'the picture deserves a respected place in the Coppola canon for various reasons, not the least of which is the host of consistently excellent performances he drew from his youthful cast' (Phillips 2010a: 197). And considering its constellation of actors, characters, and audiences, *The Outsiders* likewise deserves a respected place in the genre of teen film.

When *The Outsiders* was first released, one of the few positive reviews it received was from Gene Siskel of the *Chicago Tribune*. Calling it a 'strangely beautiful' film, Siskel concludes his review with a sincere, moving expression of gratitude: 'I will always treasure this film for the way it photographs its subjects and for the poetic words they speak' (1983: 3). Fellow fans of the movie, both young or old, feel the same way. Forty years ago, when I stepped out into the bright sunlight from the darkness of the movie house, a film had made its way into my consciousness and my heart. Since then, the same thing has happened to millions of viewers, all of whom appreciate Coppola's tender and affectionate vision of what it means to be young and gold.

Notes

1 One of the young actors who auditioned for the part of Ponyboy on the TV series was none other than the same celebrity who visited The Outsiders House Museum in 2021: Leonardo DiCaprio. While he did not land the role, he did have a bit part in the pilot.

2 For more on how queer fans potentially see themselves reflected in Hinton's story/Coppola's film, see the podcast *American Icons: The Outsiders* (2012), which briefly discusses lesbian affinities with the story, and Carter Sickels's 'Finding a More Tender, Queer Masculinity in "The Outsiders"' (2020), which examines trans identifications with the characters. Adjacent to these conversations is the ongoing dispute between Hinton and some fans regarding queer readings of the novel. A notorious argument occurred on Twitter in 2016, when a fan asked Hinton whether 'there were any romantic feelings between Johnny and Dally,' to which Hinton replied,

'No. Where is the text backing this?' From there a lengthy quarrel ensued, with Hinton defending her right to state whether her characters are gay because she is the one who created them, and others claiming (unfairly, I would argue) that Hinton's response was homophobic and that readers could interpret the characters however they wanted. See Jung (2016) and Schaub (2016) for more about this online dispute.

3 The musical was originally scheduled to debut in 2020 at the Goodman Theatre in Chicago, but that production was canceled due to the pandemic.

Bibliography

Abate, M.A. (2017) '"Soda Attracted Girls Like Honey Draws Flies": *The Outsiders*, the Boy Band Formula, and Adolescent Sexuality,' *Children's Literature Association Quarterly*, Vol. 42, No. 1, Spring, pp. 43-64.

Adair, G. (1983) 'Review of *The Outsiders*,' *Sight and Sound*, Autumn, online, republished in 'The Gilbert Adair Files,' BFI Online, http://old.bfi.org.uk/sightandsound/reviews/releases/gilbert-adair-la-luna-and-the-outsiders.php.

Amatangelo, A. (2021) '*The Outsiders: The Complete Novel*'s Restoration Proves Some Things Gold Can Stay,' *Paste*, online, 16 November, https://www.pastemagazine.com/movies/the-outsiders-complete-novel-4k-restoration/.

'American Icons: "The Outsiders"' (2012) WNYC Studies 360, online, https://www.wnyc.org/story/205279-american-icons-outsiders/.

'An Introduction to *The Outsiders: The Complete Novel* with Francis Ford Coppola' (2021), *The Outsiders: The Complete Novel* 4K edition, DVD, Warner Bros.

Ansen, D. (1983) 'Coppola Courts the Kiddies,' *Newsweek*, 4 April, p. 74.

Argetsinger, A. (2015) 'How the Brat Pack Got Its Name – and Spoiled Celebrity Journalism Forever,' *Washington Post*, online, 10 August, https://www.washingtonpost.com/news/arts-and-entertainment/wp/2015/08/10/how-the-brat-pack-got-their-name-and-spoiled-celebrity-journalism-forever/.

'Banned Book Awareness: *The Outsiders*' (2011) *World.Edu Global Education Network*, online, 8 May, https://world.edu/banned-books-awareness-outsiders/.

Baughn, N. (2018) '10 Great American Teen Films of the 1980s,' BFI Online, 7 August, https://www.bfi.org.uk/lists/10-great-american-teen-films-1980s.

Beals, S. (2018) 'Modeling Liberation: Audience, Ideology, and Critical Consciousness in S.E. Hinton's *The Outsiders*,' *Children's Literature Association Quarterly*, Vol. 43, No. 2, pp. 183-201.

Becker, T. (2018) 'The Meanings of Nostalgia: Genealogy and Critique,' *History and Theory*, Vol. 57, No. 2, June, pp. 234-250.

Bell, A. (1983) 'One from the Crotch,' *Village Voice*, 5 April, pp. 53, 93.

Bergan, R. (1997) *Francis Coppola*, New York, NY: Thunder's Mouth Press.

Blum, D. (1985) 'Hollywood's Brat Pack,' *New York*, online, 10 June, https://nymag.com/movies/features/49902/.

Blume, J. (1970) *Are You There, God? It's Me, Margaret.*, New York, NY: Dell Publishing.

Bose, P. (2021) '"The Outsiders" Is a Loving Portrayal of Young Male Vulnerability,' *The Spool*, online, 26 April, https://thespool.net/reviews/movies/the-outsiders-reveiw/.

Boym, S. (2001) *The Future of Nostalgia*, New York, NY: Basic Books.

Bradshaw, P. (2021) '*The Outsiders* Review – Coppola's Brat Pack Melodrama Carries You Away,' *Guardian*, online, 14 October, https://www.theguardian.com/film/2021/oct/14/the-outsiders-review-coppolas-brat-pack-melodrama-carries-you-away.

Brickman, B.J. (2018) *Grease: Gender, Nostalgia and Youth Consumption in the Blockbuster Era*, London: Routledge.

Buckingham, D. (n.d.) 'Introducing the JD Films,' https://davidbuckingham.net/growing-up-modern/troubling-teenagers-how-movies-constructed-the-juvenile-delinquent-in-the-1950s/introducing-the-jd-films/.

Burns, S. (2018) 'Revisiting "The Outsiders" after the Immediacy of Adolescence's Plights Have Passed,' *WBUR*, online, 31 July, https://www.wbur.org/news/2018/07/31/the-outsiders-coppola-hinton.

Camhe, T. (1983) 'A Boy's View of "Outsiders,"' *Los Angeles Times*, online, 3 April, available on *CineFiles: University of California Berkeley Art Museum & Pacific Film Archive*, https://cinefiles.bampfa.berkeley.edu/catalog/51945.

Campbell, P. (2003) '*The Outsiders*, Fat Freddy, and Me,' *Horn Book Magazine*, March/April, pp. 177-183.

Campbell, P. (1985) 'The Young Adult Perplex,' *Wilson Library Bulletin*, September, pp. 61-63.

Canby, V. (1983) '*The Outsiders*: Teen-Age Violence,' *New York Times*, 25 March, p. 18.

Carlson, B. (2018) 'Unfictional: The Outsider,' KCRW Podcast, https://www.kcrw.com/culture/shows/unfictional/the-outsider.

Cart, M. (2010) *Young Adult Literature: From Romance to Realism*, Chicago. IL: American Library Association.

Cart, M. (2001) 'From Insider to Outsiders: The Evolution of Young Adult Literature,' *Voices from the Middle*, Vol. 9, No. 2, December, pp. 95-97.

Chaillet, J. and Vincent, E. (1984) *Francis Ford Coppola*, New York, NY: St. Martin's Press (trans. D. Raab Jacobs).

Chambers, A. (1970) 'Review of *The Outsiders*,' *Children's Book News*, Vol. 5, No. 6, November/December, p. 280.

Chown, J. (1988) *Hollywood Auteur: Francis Coppola*, Westport, CT: Praeger.

Christie, T.A. (2009) *John Hughes and Eighties Cinema: Teenage Hopes and American Dreams*, Kent (UK): Crescent Moon.

Coats, K. (2011) 'Growing Up, In Theory,' in S. Wolf, K. Coats, P. Enciso, and C. Jenkins (eds) *Handbook of Research on Children's and Young Adult Literature*, New York, NY: Routledge, pp. 315-329.

Considine, D.M. (1985) *The Cinema of Adolescence*, Jefferson, NC: McFarland.

Corliss, R. (1983) 'Playing Tough, Going Nowhere,' *Time*, 4 April, p. 78.

Cowie, P. (1989) *Coppola*, New York, NY: Charles Scribner's Sons.

Coyle, J. (2005) 'Coppola Returns to *The Outsiders*,' *Sarasota Herald Tribune*, online, 8 September, https://www.heraldtribune.com/story/news/2005/09/08/coppola-returns-to-the-outsiders/28861580007/.

Daly, J. (1989) *Presenting S.E. Hinton*, Updated Edition, Boston, MA: Twayne Publishers.

Dargis, M. (2005) 'Coppola Pays a Return Visit to His "Gone With the Wind" for Teenagers,' *New York Times*, online, 9 September, https://www.nytimes.com/2005/09/09/movies/coppola-pays-a-return-visit-to-his-gone-with-the-wind-for-teenagers.html.

Davis, F. (1979) *Yearning for Yesterday: A Sociology of Nostalgia*, New York, NY: The Free Press.

Denby, D. (1983) 'Romance for Boys,' *New York*, 4 April, pp. 73-74.

Doherty, T. (2002) *Teenagers and Teenpics: The Juvenilization of American Movies in the 1950s*, Revised and Expanded Edition, Philadelphia, PA: Temple University Press.

'Domestic Grosses: *The Outsiders*' (2022) *BoxOfficeMojo*, online, https://www.boxofficemojo.com/release/rl1953072641/weekend/.

'Domestic Box Office for 1983' (n.d.) *BoxOfficeMojo*, online, https://www.boxofficemojo.com/year/1983/.

'Domestic Box Office for 1982' (n.d.) *BoxOfficeMojo*, online, https://www.boxofficemojo.com/year/1982/.

Driscoll, C. (2011) *Teen Film: A Critical Introduction*, New York, NY: Berg Publishers.

Duffett, M. (2013) *Understanding Fandom: An Introduction to the Study of Media Fan Culture*, New York, NY: Bloomsbury.

Dunham, L. (2018) 'The Enduring Spell of "The Outsiders,"' *New York Times Style Magazine*, online, 5 September, https://www.nytimes.com/2018/09/05/t-magazine/outsiders-book-hinton-lena-dunham.html.

Dwyer, M.D. (2015) *Back to the Fifties: Nostalgia, Hollywood Film, and Popular Music of the Seventies and Eighties*, Oxford: Oxford University Press.

Ebert, R. (1983a) 'Interview with Matt Dillon,' *RogerEbert.com*, online, 24 April, https://www.rogerebert.com/interviews/interview-with-matt-dillon.

Ebert, R. (1983b) 'Review of *The Outsiders*,' *RogerEbert.com*, online, 25 March, https://www.rogerebert.com/reviews/the-outsiders-1983.

Eby, M. (2017) 'Why *The Outsiders* Still Matters,' *Rolling Stone*, online, 26 April, https://www.rollingstone.com/feature/why-the-outsiders-still-matters-50-years-later-194014/.

Ehrlich, L. (1981) 'Advice from a Penwoman,' *Seventeen*, November, p. 32.

Elsaesser, T. (1987) 'Tales of Sound and Fury: Observations on the Family Melodrama,' in C. Gledhill (ed) *Home Is Where the Heart Is: Studies in Melodrama and the Woman's Film*, London: BFI Publishing, pp. 43-68 (originally published in 1972).

Ethington, T. (2021) 'Stay Gold, Danny Boy,' *Rolling Stone*, online, 5 November, https://www.rollingstone.com/tv-movies/tv-movie-features/outsiders-movie-house-museum-danny-boy-house-of-pain-1220618/.

Farber, S. (1983) 'Directors Join the S.E. Hinton Fan Club,' *New York Times*, online, 20 March, https://www.nytimes.com/1983/03/20/movies/directors-join-the-se-hinton-fan-club.html.

'*Fast Times at Ridgemont High*: Summary' (n.d.) *The Numbers*, online, https://www.the-numbers.com/movie/Fast-Times-at-Ridgemont-High#tab=summary.

Fellwock, M. (2021) Interview with the author, 19 July.

Fleming, T. (1967) 'Review of *The Outsiders*,' *New York Times Book Review*, 7 May, pp. 10, 12.

Freeman, H. (2015) *Life Moves Pretty Fast: The Lessons We Learned from Eighties Movies (and Why We Don't Learn Them from Movies Anymore)*, New York, NY: Simon and Schuster Paperbacks.

Gelmis, R. (1983) 'Rebels with Causes,' *Newsday*, 25 March, p. 151.

Gerhardt, L.N. (1967) 'Review of *The Outsiders*,' *School Library Journal*, 9 May, pp. 64-65.

'Gian-Carlo Coppola: Filmography' (n.d.) *IMDb.com*, online, https://m.imdb.com/name/nm0178887/filmotype?ref_=m_nm_flmg.

Gilliam, M., Kline, J., O'Shansky, J., and Wright, M. (2016) 'Making "The Outsiders": Cast and Crew Share Memories of the Film Production,' *Tulsa People*, online, 3 August, https://www.tulsapeople.com/the-voice/writers/mitch-gilliam/making-the-outsiders/article_c1093ea9-db3c-580e-9178-a9025346cad8.html.

Gledhill, C. (ed)(1987a) *Home Is Where the Heart Is: Studies in Melodrama and the Woman's Film*, London: BFI Publishing.

Gledhill, C. (1987b) 'The Melodramatic Field: An Investigation,' in C. Gledhill (ed) *Home Is Where the Heart Is: Studies in Melodrama and the Woman's Film*, London: BFI Publishing, pp. 5-39.

Godfrey, A. (2021) 'Ganging Up,' *Empire Magazine*, November, pp. 96-101.

Gora, S. (2010) *You Couldn't Ignore Me If You Tried: The Brat Pack, John Hughes, and Their Impact on a Generation*, New York, NY: Three Rivers Press.

Graham, G. (2017) 'Forever an Outsider: Tulsa Author S.E. Hinton Looks Back 50 Years to Her First Book,' *Tulsa World*, online, 5 May, https://tulsaworld.com/lifestyles/magazine/forever-an-outsider-tulsa-author-s-e-hinton-looks-back-50-years-to-her-first/article_ce9a7027-c470-50f3-82f0-3a993cd2f768.html.

Green, J. (2014) *The Fault in Our Stars*, New York, NY: Penguin Books.

Harmetz, A. (1983) 'Making *The Outsiders:* A Librarian's Dream,' *New York Times*, online, 23 March, https://www.nytimes.com/1983/03/23/movies/making-the-outsiders-a-librarian-s-dream.html.

Harper, S. (n.d.) 'Melodrama: Torrid Passions and Doomed Desires,' *BFI Screen Online*, http://www.screenonline.org.uk/film/id/446129/index.html.

Hentoff, N. (1968) 'Fiction for Teen-agers,' *Wilson Library Bulletin*, November, pp. 261-265.

Hills, M. (2013) 'Foreword: What If? Reimagining Fandom,' in M. Duffett (ed) *Understanding Fandom*, New York, NY: Bloomsbury, pp. vi-xii.

Hills, M. (2002) *Fan Cultures*, London: Routledge.

Hinton, S.E. (1967a) *The Outsiders*, New York: Speak-Putnam Penguin Inc.

Hinton, S.E. (1967b) 'Teen-Agers Are for Real,' *New York Times*, 27 August, pp. 26-29.

Hirshenson, J., and Jenkins, J., with Krantz, R. (2006) *A Star Is Found: Our Adventures Casting Some of Hollywood's Biggest Movies*, Orlando, FL: Harcourt, Inc.

Hoad, P. (2021) '"Tom Cruise Was an Intense Kid": How Francis Ford Coppola Made *The Outsiders*,' *Guardian*, online, 1 November, https://www.theguardian.com/film/2021/nov/01/how-we-made-the-outsiders-francis-ford-coppola-and-c-thomas-howell.

Holyfield, L., Cobb, M., Murray, K., and McKinzie A. (2013) 'Musical Ties That Bind: Nostalgia, Affect, and Heritage in Festival Narratives,' *Symbolic Interaction*, Vol. 36, No. 4, pp. 457-477.

Howard, T. (2001) *Understanding* The Outsiders, San Diego, CA: Lucent Books.

Hutcheon, L. (2000) 'Irony, Nostalgia, and the Postmodern,' in R. Vervliet and A. Estor (eds) *Methods for the Study of Literature as Cultural Memory*, Amsterdam: Rodopi, pp. 189-207.

Inderbitzin, M. (2003) 'Outsiders and Justice Consciousness,' *Contemporary Justice Review*, Vol. 6, No. 4, pp. 357-362.

Jay, R. (2022) 'The Outsiders,' *Television Obscurities: Exploring Forgotten TV From the 1920s to Today*, https://www.tvobscurities.com/articles/outsiders/.

Jensen, K. (2020) 'Go Global with These (Nearly) 80 YA Books Set around the World,' *BookRiot.com*, online, 16 March, https://bookriot.com/ya-books-set-around-the-world/.

Johnson, C.D. (2004) *Youth Gangs in Literature*, Westport, CT: Greenwood Press.

Johnston, S. (1983) 'Review of *The Outsiders*,' *Film Monthly Bulletin*, September, BFI Programme Notes, https://bfidatadigipres.github.io/re-releases/2021/10/22/outisders-complete-novel/.

Jones, S.J. (2012) 'The Life and Works of S.E. Hinton,' in D. Nelson (ed) *Teen Issues in S.E. Hinton's* The Outsiders, Detroit, MI: Gale Cengage Learning, pp. 16-29 (originally published in 2000).

Jung, E.A. (2016) 'S.E. Hinton: No, *The Outsiders* Didn't Have Any Gay Lovers,' *Vulture*, online, 16 October, https://www.vulture.com/2016/10/se-hinton-no-the-outsiders-arent-gay-lovers.html.

Kakutani, M. (1984) 'What Is Hollywood Saying about the Teen-Age World Today?' *New York Times*, 22 April, pp. H1, H22.

Kemply, R. (1983) '"The Outsiders": Greaser Gospel,' *Washington Post*, online, 25 March, https://www.washingtonpost.com/archive/lifestyle/1983/03/25/the-outsiders-greaser-gospel/aee3114d-daa0-4f39-b66d-20034892a780/.

Kennedy, M. (2021) 'Which 1980s Teen Stars Were Members of the Brat Pack?' *Screen Rant*, online, 6 November, https://screenrant.com/brat-pack-actors-members-teen-stars/.

King, D. (2019) 'Matt Dillon – This Era's James Dean,' *Tulsa World*, online, 23 February, https://tulsaworld.com/archive/matt-dillon—this-eras-james-dean-drugstore-cowboy-star-takes-critics-award-speculation/article_35b3babd-7679-52ff-b382-2daffe6ab4ad.html (originally published 12 January 1990).

King, J. (2018) *Fast Times and Excellent Adventures: The Surprising History of the '80s Teen Movie*, London: Constable.

King, S. (2018) '"The Outsiders" Stays Gold at 35: Inside Coppola's Crafty Methods and Stars' Crazy Pranks,' *Variety*, online, 23 March, https://variety.com/2018/film/news/the-outsiders-oral-history-francis-ford-coppola-ralph-macchio-diane-lane-1202732109/.

Klein, A.A. (2011) *American Film Cycles: Reframing Genres, Screening Social Problems, and Defining Subcultures*, Austin, TX: University of Texas Press.

Kolbert. E. (1994) 'The Slump in Teen Idoldom,' *New York Times: Styles*, 7 August, pp. 45, 48.

Korfhage, M. (2017) '*Outsiders* Author S.E. Hinton Talks Matt Dillon, and Why Everybody Keeps Showing Her Their Tattoo,' *Willamette Weekly*, online, 16 May, https://www.wweek.com/uncategorized/2017/05/16/outsiders-author-s-e-hinton-talks-matt-dillon-and-why-everybody-keeps-showing-her-their-tattos/.

Krischer, H. (2017) 'Why "The Outsiders" Lives On: A Teenage Novel Turns 50,' *New York Times*, online, 12 March, https://www.nytimes.com/2017/03/12/books/the-outsiders-s-e-hinton-book.html.

Landsberg, M. (1987) *Reading for the Love of It: Best Books for Young Readers*, New York, NY: Prentice Hall Press.

Lasch, C. (1984) 'The Politics of Nostalgia,' *Harper's*, November, pp. 65-70.

Lebeau, V. (1995) *Lost Angels: Psychoanalysis and Cinema*, London: Routledge.

Lewis, J. (1995) *Whom God Wishes to Destroy....:Francis Coppola and the New Hollywood*, Durham, NC: Duke University Press.

Lewis, J. (1992) *The Road to Romance and Ruin: Teen Films and Youth Culture*, New York, NY: Routledge.

Lewis, M. (2016) 'The Rumble of Nostalgia: Francis Ford Coppola's Vision of Boyhood,' *Boyhood Studies*, Vol. 9, No. 1, March, pp. 6-21.

Loewenthal, D. (1985) *The Past Is a Foreign Country*, Cambridge: Cambridge University Press.

Loughrey, C. (2020) 'The Brat Pack: Their 10 Greatest Films, from *The Breakfast Club* to *Sixteen Candles*, *Independent*, online, 6 June, https://www.independent.co.uk/arts-entertainment/films/features/the-brat-pack-the-breakfast-club-sixteen-candles-john-hughes-emilio-estevez-molly-ringwald-a9549326.html.

Lowe, R. (2011) *Stories I Only Tell My Friends*, New York, NY: St. Martin's Press.

Lyman, R. (1983) 'Without Fanfare, Coppola Triumphs with *Outsiders*,' *Philadelphia Inquirer*, 26 March, pp. 1D, 3D.

Macnab, G. (2021) 'Testosterone-driven Action Meets Dreamy Interludes: How *The Outsiders* Launched the Careers of the Brat Pack,' *Independent*, online, 7 May, https://www.independent.co.uk/independentpremium/culture/the-outsiders-francis-ford-coppola-brat-back-b1843005.html.

'Matt Dillon Countdown Part One' (1983) *16 Magazine*, February, pp. 23-24.

'Matt Dillon: Don't Believe ALL You Read!' (1983) *16 Magazine*, April, pp. 28-29.

'Matt Dillon's Private Life!' (1983) *16 Magazine*, March, pp. 10-11.

'Matt, Tom & Ralph Will Make You Cry In "The Outsiders!"' (1982) *Tiger Beat Star*, December, pp. 54-55.

Mazer, J. (2018) 'New Illusion: *The Outsiders, Rumble Fish*, and Coppola in the Early '80s,' *Bryn Mawr Film Institute*, online, https://medium.com/bryn-mawr-film-institute/new-illusion-the-outsiders-rumble-fish-and-coppola-in-the-early-'80s-e6a0fa3f2e95.

McCarthy, T. (1982) 'WB Gets Coppola's *Outsiders*; Teenage Pic Eyes Fall Bow,' *Variety*, 17 March, pp. 6, 172.

McCormick, A.A. (1989) '*The Outsiders*,' in K.H. Beetz and S. Niemeyer (eds) *Beacham's Guide to Literature for Young Adults*, Volume 2, Ann Arbor, MI: University of Michigan Press, pp. 1007-1014.

Mercer, J. and Shingler, M. (2004) *Melodrama: Genre, Style, Sensibility*, London: Wallflower.

Merritt, R. (1983) 'Melodrama: Postmortem for a Phantom Genre,' *Wide Angle*, Vol. 5, No. 3, pp. 24-31.

Michaud, J. (2014) 'S.E. Hinton and the Y.A. Debate,' *New Yorker*, online, 14 October, https://www.newyorker.com/culture/cultural-comment/hinton-outsiders-young-adult-literature.

Misakian, J.E. (2021) Interview with the author, 2 September.

Mockoski, J. (2021) Interview with the author, 25 August.

Mulvey, L. (1999) 'Visual Pleasure and Narrative Cinema,' in L. Braudy and M. Cohen (eds) *Film Theory and Criticism: Introductory Readings*, New York, NY: Oxford University Press, pp. 833-844 (originally published in 1975).

Nash, I. (2003) 'Hysterical Scream or Rebel Yell? The Politics of Teen-Idol Fandom,' in S. Inness (ed) *Disco Divas: Women and Popular Culture in the 1970s*, Philadelphia, PA: University of Pennsylvania Press, pp. 133-150.

Nashville Film Institute (n.d.) 'Two Shot,' online, https://www.nfi.edu/two-shot-s234-backup/.

Neale, S. (1986) 'Melodrama and Tears,' *Screen*, Vol. 27, No. 6, November-December, pp. 6-23.

Nelson, E.H. (2019) *The Breakfast Club: John Hughes, Hollywood, and the Golden Age of the Teen Film*, New York, NY: Routledge.

Nodelman, P. (1986) 'Teaching Girls about Men: Attitudes toward Maleness in Teen Magazines,' *Studies in Popular Culture*, Vol. 9, No. 1, pp. 103-118.

O'Connor, D. (2021) Interview with the author, 12 July.

'100 "Most Inspiring" Novels Revealed by BBC Arts' (2019) *BBC*, online, 5 November, https://www.bbc.com/news/entertainment-arts-50302788.

O'Toole, L. (1983) 'Rebels without a Cause,' *Macleans*, 4 April, p. 62.

'*Outsiders* Review! What You Thought! What the Stars Felt! What the Critics Said!' (1983) *16 Magazine*, August, pp. 4-9.

Pallister, K. (2019) 'Introduction,' in K. Pallister (ed) *Netflix Nostalgia: Streaming the Past on Demand*, Lanham, MD: Lexington Books, pp. 1-7.

Peck, D. (2007) '*The Outsiders*: 40 Years Later,' *New York Times Book Review*, 23 September, p. 31.

Peck, R. (1993) 'The Silver Anniversary of Young Adult Books,' *Journal of Youth Services in Libraries*, Fall, pp. 19-23.

Peck, R. (1972) *Don't Look and It Won't Hurt*, New York, NY: Henry Holt and Company.

Peters, A. (n.d.) 'Who Buys on Etsy? Audience and Demographics (Statistics),' *Techpenny.com*, online, https://techpenny.com/typical-etsy-demographics-stats/.

Phillips, G.D. (2010a) '*The Outsiders* (1983),' in J. Welsh, G.D. Phillips, and R. Hill (eds) *The Francis Ford Coppola Encyclopedia*, Lanham, MD: Scarecrow Press, pp. 194-198.

Phillips, G.D. (2010b) '*The Outsiders: Expanded Version* (2005),' in J. Welsh, G.D. Phillips, and R. Hill (eds) *The Francis Ford Coppola Encyclopedia*, Lanham, MD: Scarecrow Press, pp. 198-199.

Phillips, G. D. (2004) *Godfather: The Intimate Francis Ford Coppola*, Lexington, KY: University Press of Kentucky.

Profitt, B. (2020) 'He Appeared […] Clad Only in a Pair of Low-Cut Blue Jeans:" Incipient Female Gazing at *The Outsiders* (1983),' *#WaynePop*, online, 22 September, https://s.wayne.edu/waynepop/2020/09/22/blue-profitt/.

Pulliam, J. (2012) '*The Outsiders* Offers a Nuanced Critique of Class Mobility and Gender Identity,' in D. Nelson (ed) *Teen Issues in S.E. Hinton's* The Outsiders, Detroit, MI: Gale Cengage Learning, pp. 79-91 (originally published in 2010).

Rabin, N. (2015) '*The Outsiders* Television Pilot Isn't Quite Golden,' *The Dissolve*, online, 6 February, https://thedissolve.com/news/4695-the-outsiders-television-pilot-isnt-quite-golden/.

'Ralph Macchio: What Turns Him On... & Off!' (1983) *16 Magazine*, March, pp. 64-65.

Ramsey, N. (2005) 'An Ageless Shot at Redemption: *The Outsiders* Touched Francis Ford Coppola at a Time When His Future Looked Bleak,' *Los Angeles Times*, 18 September, p. E14.

Rees, D. (1984) 'Macho Man, American Style,' in *Painted Desert, Green Shade*, Boston, MA: The Horn Book Inc., pp. 126-137.

'Review of *The Outsiders*' (1967), *Kirkus Review*, 15 April, pp. 506-507.

'Review of *The Outsiders*' (1970) *Times Literary Supplement (TLS)*, 30 October, p. 1258.

'Review of *The Outsiders*' (1983) *Variety*, 23 March, p. 18.

Rice, L. (2021) 'An Oral History of *The Outsiders*,' *Entertainment Weekly*, online, https://ew.com/movies/the-outsiders-oral-history/.

'Roman Coppola: Filmography' (n.d.) *IMDb.com*, online, https://m.imdb.com/name/nm0178910/filmotype?ref_=m_nm_flmg.

Ross, L. (2004) 'Some Figures on a Fantasy: Francis Coppola,' in G.D. Phillips and R. Hill (eds) *Francis Ford Coppola: Interviews*, Jackson, MS: University Press of Mississippi, pp. 63-105 (originally published in 1982).

Routledge, C., Wildschut, T., Sedikides, C., Juhl, J., and Arndt, J. (2012) 'The Power of the Past: Nostalgia as a Meaning-Making Resource,' *Memory*, Vol. 20, No. 5, May, pp. 452-460.

Ryan, M. and Kellner, D. (1988) *Camera Politica: The Politics and Ideology of Contemporary Hollywood Film*, Bloomington and Indianapolis, IN: Indiana University Press.

Salmose, N. (2019) 'Nostalgia Makes Us All Tick: A Special Issue on Contemporary Nostalgia,' *Humanities*, Vol. 8, No. 3, pp. 1-5.

Sarris, A. (1983) 'Review of *The Outsiders*,' *Village Voice*, 5 April, available on *CineFiles: University of California Berkeley Art Museum & Pacific Film Archive*, https://cinefiles.bampfa.berkeley.edu/catalog/51934.

Schatz, T. (1981) *Hollywood Genres: Formula, Filmmaking, and the Studio System*, New York, NY: Random House.

Schaub, M. (2016) '"The Outsiders" Author S.E. Hinton Is in Hot Water with Gay-Rights Supporters,' *Los Angeles Times*, online, 19 October, https://www.latimes.com/books/jacketcopy/la-et-jc-outsiders-gay-20161019-snap-story.html.

Schumacher, M. (1999) *Francis Ford Coppola: A Filmmaker's Life*, New York, NY: Crown Publishers.

Seay, E.A. (2012) 'Opulence to Decadence: *The Outsiders* and *Less Than Zero*,' in D. Nelson, (ed) *Teen Issues in S.E. Hinton's* The Outsiders, Detroit, MI: Gale Cengage Learning, pp. 92-99 (originally published in 1987).

Shanofsky, R. (2021) Interview with the author, 26 July.

Shary, T. (2022) Email to the author, 18 January.

Shary, T. (2014) *Generation Multiplex: The Image of Youth in American Cinema since 1980*, Revised Edition, Austin, TX: University of Texas Press.

Shary, T. (2005) *Teen Movies: American Youth on Screen*, New York, NY: Wallflower.

Sickels, C. (2020) 'Finding a More Tender, Queer Masculinity in "The Outsiders,"' *Catapult*, online, 24 June, https://catapult.co/stories/finding-a-more-tender-queer-masculinity-in-the-outsiders-journey-transgender-masculinity-ralph-macchio-carter-sickels.

Siskel, G. (1983) 'Coppola Gets Inside Real Teen World to Film a Noble Story of "Outsiders,"' *Chicago Tribune*, 25 March, Section 3, p. 3.

'16 Magazine' (n.d.) *Nostalgia Central: The Way Things Used to Be*, https://nostalgiacentral.com/pop-culture/fads/16-magazine/.

Shelton, J. (n.d.) 'Teen Magazines of the '60 and '70s: Mad about The Boys!,' *Groovy History*, online, https://groovyhistory.com/16-magazine-tiger-beat-teen-60s-70s/8.

Smith, F. (2017) *Rethinking the Hollywood Teen Movie: Gender, Genre and Identity*, Edinburgh: Edinburgh University Press.

'Sofia Coppola: Filmography' (n.d.) *IMBd.com*, online, https://m.imdb.com/name/nm0001068/filmotype?ref_=m_nm_flmg.

Sragow, M. (1983) '*The Outsiders*: Coppola Gives Adolescence a Bad Name,' *Rolling Stone*, 12 May, p. 55.

Stack, P. (1983) 'Teen Gangs Take Over the Movies This Week,' *San Francisco Chronicle*, 25 March, p. 62.

Starobinski, J. (1966) 'The Idea of Nostalgia,' *Diogenes*, Vol. 14, No. 54, pp. 81-103 (trans. W.S. Kemp).

'Staying Gold: A Look Back at "The Outsiders"' (2005) *The Outsiders: The Complete Novel*, Dir. Kim Aubrey, DVD, Warner Bros.

Sutherland, Z. (1968) 'The Teen-Ager Speaks,' *Saturday Review*, 27 January, p. 34.

Sutherland, Z. (1967) 'Review of *The Outsiders*,' *Saturday Review*, 13 May, p. 59.

Tannock, S. (1995) 'Nostalgia Critique,' *Cultural Studies*, Vol. 9, No. 3, pp. 453-464.

'The Making of *The Outsiders* Part 1' (1982) *16 Magazine*, August, pp. 6-9.

'The Making of *The Outsiders* Part 2' (1982) *16 Magazine*, September, pp. 8-11.

'The Making of *The Outsiders* Part 3' (1982) *16 Magazine*, October, pp. 30-33.

'The Making of *The Outsiders* Part 4' (1982) *16 Magazine*, November, pp. 15-18.

'The Making of *The Outsiders* Part 5' (1982) *16 Magazine*, December, pp. 15-18.

'The Making of *The Outsiders* Part 6' (1983) *16 Magazine*, January, pp. 6-9.

'*The Outsiders* Is Coming!' (1982) *16 Magazine*, July, pp. 17-18.

Thomas, A. (2017) *The Hate U Give*, Balzer + Bray-HarperCollins Publishers.

Thomson, D. and Gray, L. (1983) 'Idols of the King: *The Outsiders* and *Rumble Fish*,' *Film Comment*, September/October, Vol. 19, No. 5, pp. 61-75.

'Tommy Howell Fact File!' (1983) *16 Magazine*, February, pp. 30-31.

'Tommy Howell: The Most Unusual Boy You've Ever Met!' (1983) *16 Magazine*, January, pp. 26-27.

Town, C.J. (2014) '*Unsuitable' Books: Young Adult Fiction and Censorship*, Jefferson, NC: McFarland & Company.

Tribunella, E.L. (2010) *Melancholia and Maturation: The Use of Trauma in American Children's Literature*, Knoxville, TN: University of Tennessee Press.

Turan, K. (1983) 'Class Struggles,' *California Magazine*, May, pp. 120-121.

Wallis, C. (1982) 'Dillon's Promise,' *Rolling Stone*, 27 November, pp. 14, 87.

Wells, J. (1983) 'Review of *The Outsiders*,' *Film Journal International*, 15 April, p. 35.

Whissen, T.R. (1992) *Classic Cult Fiction: A Companion to Popular Cult Literature*, Westport, CT: Greenwood Press, pp. 184-190.

White, A. (1985) 'Kidpix,' *Film Comment*, July/August, pp. 9-15.

Williams, L. (1998) 'Melodrama Revised,' in N. Browne (ed) *Refiguring American Film Genres: Theory and History*, Berkeley, CA: University of California Press, pp. 42-88.

Wilson, J.L. (2015) 'Here and Now, There and Then: Nostalgia as a Time and Space Phenomenon,' *Symbolic Interaction*, Vol. 38, No. 3, November, pp. 478-492.

Wilson, J.L. (1999) '"REMEMBER WHEN...": A Consideration of the Concept of Nostalgia,' *ETC: A Review of General Semantics*, Vol. 56, No. 3, Fall, pp. 296-304.

Winter, L. (2022) 'Death by Nostalgia, 1688,' *The Scientist*, online, 1 February, https://www.the-scientist.com/foundations/death-by-nostalgia-1688-69596.

Wistisen, L. (2021) 'Too Much Feeling: S.E. Hinton's *The Outsiders* (1967), Conflicting Emotions, Identity, and Socialization,' *Children's Literature in Education*, No. 52, pp. 200-216.

Wood, D. (1994) 'Outside of Nothing: The Place of Community in *The Outsiders*,' in S.C. Aiken and L.E. Zonn (eds) *Power, Place, Situation, and Spectacle: A Geography of Film*, Lanham, MD: Rowman & Littlefield Publishers, Inc., pp. 101-118.

Wojciechowska, M. (1968) 'An End to Nostalgia,' *School Library Journal*, December, pp. 13-15.

Zacharek, S. (2007) 'Adult Themes,' *New York Times Book Review*, online, 13 May, https://www.nytimes.com/2007/05/13/books/review/Zacharek-t.html.

Index

Note: page numbers in italics indicate figures.

For Product Safety Concerns and Information please contact our EU
representative GPSR@taylorandfrancis.com
Taylor & Francis Verlag GmbH, Kaufingerstraße 24, 80331 München, Germany

www.ingramcontent.com/pod-product-compliance
Lightning Source LLC
Chambersburg PA
CBHW060547310726
48982CB00012B/114

* 9 7 8 1 0 3 2 1 3 3 3 8 6 *